B

Runaway Fever

Black Dress Trilogy Volume 1

by

Kenneth James Taylor

TELEMACHUS PRESS

RUNAWAY FEVER: BLACK DRESS TRILOGY VOLUME ONE

Cover Designed by Telemachus Press, LLC

Cover art:
Copyright © iStockphoto/6730563
Copyright © iStockphoto/15679863
Copyright © iStockphoto/22946879

Published by Telemachus Press, LLC
http://www.telemachuspress.com

Visit the author website:
http://kennethjamestaylor.com

ISBN: 978-1-939337-79-5 (eBook)
ISBN: 978-1-939927-39-2 (Paperback)

Version 2013.06.07

Printed in the United States of America

10 9 8 7 6 5 4 3 2 1

Black Dress Trilogy contains no obscenity or foul language. However, it does contain violence as might have occurred during the 1836 Texas Revolution. The trilogy is presented in the following three volumes:

Volume 1: Runaway Fever
Molly McCracken's husband does not return from the war. She flees unprepared with her beloved sister from the onslaught of the 1836 invasion of Texas. Along the boggy road to safety her friends and neighbors bury their loved ones where they fall. Attempting to save her niece, she risks it all and fails. Her life spins out of control and her survival becomes uncertain until a Ranger tries to help.

Volume 2: Tuck's Landing
Molly McCracken rebuilds her life and meets a colorful new friend who sooths the agony of her loss. Determined to find her niece she struggles to keep from falling in love with the man who saved her life during the war. She knows she must learn to fight. Then an altercation lands her in the most dangerous town in Texas where she cleverly improves the lives of the innocent children she encounters.

Volume 3: Call of the Grackle
Molly McCracken confronts a corrupt madam, outsmarts a crooked store owner, and pursues a gang of infamous smugglers to free those in bondage. Then a mysterious bit of information sweeps her into the wilderness and plunges her into a conflict that binds her to her soul mate. Will she follow her heart and betroth herself to the man she loves or will she continue to search for her missing husband?

RUNAWAY FEVER SYNOPSIS

The tragic flight of the refugees during the Texas Revolution is depicted as accurately as possible when Molly McCracken and her sister flee unprepared with their friends and neighbors from the 1836 invasion of Texas by Mexico. Molly's husband joins the fight and does not return. She fears that he is dead. Along the boggy Atascosito Road the refugees bury their loved ones where they fall as victims of depredation, perilous weather conditions, famine and disease. Close behind, Santa Anna vows to execute every man, woman and child in Texas, destroy their homes and leave nothing for them to return to should they survive. The journey is difficult but not impossible. In an attempt to save her niece, Molly risks it all and fails. Her life spins out of control and her survival becomes uncertain until a Texas Ranger tries to help.

Table of Contents

Map of the Black Dress Trilogy	i
Trilogy Characters	ii
Trilogy Places	vi
Trilogy Words and Phrases	viii
Trilogy Acknowledgements	xi
Forward to the Black Dress Trilogy	xiii
Preface to the Black Dress Trilogy	xvii
Prologue: The Attic	1
Runaway Fever	5
The Dream	18
Oscar	28
Root Hog or Die	36
San Felipe	47
Missis Powell's Tavern	59
Rice Water	68
Sugar Lead	75
Matagorda	87
Buffalo Head	97
The Thicket	110
The Blackberry Patch	125
The Brazos	137
Epilogue: Too Much Excitement	149
Selections from ***Tuck's Landing: Black Dress Trilogy Volume 2***	151

MAP OF THE BLACK DRESS TRILOGY

TRILOGY CHARACTERS

Adama: fictitious middle-aged former slave woman

Alsey: fictitious Texas Ranger serving under Captain Boots Williams

Arnwine: fictitious doctor in San Antonio who attends Texas Rangers wounded in skirmishes

Banish: fictitious owner of a mercantile in Nacogdoches, and a competitor of Hoxie's General Mercantile

Benson, Maria and five boys: fictitious secondary character, flees with Molly and other refugees from Santa Anna and re-emerges in the story while returning to Gonzales

Biladeau, Christiana: fictitious representative of Bildad from the *Book of Job*, encounters Molly at Missis Powell's Tavern

Buffalo Head: fictitious secondary character of Mexican-Indian decent, trader, smuggler, ally of Santa Anna, known by Texas settlers as a land pirate, outlaw or bandit

Carrigan, Emily, husband Innis, and daughter Amy: fictitious character, Emily is Molly's sister, and flees with her and other refugees from the invading army of Santa Anna

Casey, Colonel Martin: fictitious Indian agent for the Republic of Texas

Córdova, Vicente: District Prosecutor for District of Nacogdoches

Doyle: fictitious Texas Ranger serving under Captain Boots Williams

Fannin, Commander: defeated by the Garza rancheros in the area of Goliad, he was again defeated by General Urrea at Coleto Creek, and was executed with the remainder of his forces at the presidio in Goliad on Palm Sunday

Folkvar, Klaus: fictitious ferryboat operator for Aunt Ruthie at Tuck's Landing

Garza rancheros: allied with Santa Anna, they banded together against Commander Fannin and his forces in the area of Goliad

Hamadi: former slave, husband to Adama, and is captured by John A. Murrell

Hodge, Arlan: fictitious Texas Ranger assigned to Fort Casey near Nacogdoches, formerly rode with Captain Boots Williams

Hort, Henry: fictitious neighbor to Molly, flees with her and other refugees from Santa Anna, and re-emerges in the story while returning to Gonzales

Houston, General Samuel: leads Texan army against the invading army of Santa Anna, and orders Gonzales burned

Hoxie, Dugan, Mrs. Hoxie, and son Jeffery: fictitious owners and operators of Hoxie's General Mercantile in Nacogdoches

Justin: fictitious farmhand for Aunt Ruthie at Tuck's Landing

Karnes, Colonel: stationed in San Antonio, commands the Texas Rangers in the southwest territories, and is Captain Boots Williams' superior officer

King Ghezo of Dahomey: deposes Adama's royal family in Africa and sells her into slavery

LaMonte, Herman, and Madam Fredericka: fictitious plantation owners in Louisiana where Molly's sister, Emily, worked as a seamstress

Manuel: farmhand for Aunt Ruthie at Tuck's Landing

McClellan, Asa: Texas Ranger serving under Captain Boots Williams

McCracken, Emmet: husband of Molly McCracken

McCracken, Molly: main character and diary writer who flees with other refugees from the invading army of Santa Anna

Milliken: fictitious plantation from which Adama and Hadami obtain freedom

Mora, Juan: Judge for the District of Nacogdoches

Murrell, John A.: historic criminal and slave smuggler

Noah: fictitious Texas Ranger serving under Captain Boots Williams

Nomusha: fictitious adolescent slave and victim of slave theft

Owen, Margaret, children Callie and Toby: fictitious characters dispossessed by war, Margaret is forced into prostitution, and her children are abandoned

Pallet, Sam: fictitious de facto owner of Fort Teran

Phipps, Pastor Eli: fictitious circuit preacher representative of Eliphaz from the *Book of Job*, encounters Molly in San Felipe

Powell, Missis: owns tavern serving travelers at a southern Texas crossroad, assists Molly and her family when they are in distress

Santa Anna: President of Mexico, attempts to drive American settlers out of Texas by leading invasion

Sarah: fictitious housemaid serving the LaMonte plantation

Santo Muerte: Saint of Death worshiped in parts of Texas

Schauble, Titus and Annie: fictitious elderly owners of mercantile in Gonzales before it is burned, they flee with Molly and other refugees from Santa Anna

Susser, Elli-Lou, and husband Franklin: fictitious representative of Elihu from the *Book of Job*, neighbor and close friend of Molly, flees with her and other refugees from Santa Anna, and re-emerges in story while returning to Gonzales

Thaxton, Zacharias: fictitious Texas Ranger serving under Captain Boots Williams

Timble, R.C.: Chief Surveyor, Bexar District, San Antonio

Travis, Colonel: writes letter asking for help to defend the Alamo

Tuck, Aunt Ruthie, and deceased husband Foster: fictitious owner and manager of Tuck's Landing, a boarding house and ferryboat crossing at the Trinidad River near Liberty, Texas, she is the aunt of Captain Boots Williams

Uncle Elmer: fictitious relative of Elli-Lou Susser

Uriel: canonical Archangel prior to exclusion from veneration in AD 745, formerly considered one of the Archangels of the four winds including Gabriel, Michael, and Raphael

Urrea, General: served Santa Anna, invaded southern Texas and the coast

Williams, Avery and Elizabeth: fictitious father and mother of Captain Boots Williams, both deceased, Elizabeth was sister of Aunt Ruthie Tuck

Williams, Captain Boots: fictitious main character, born Francis Jacob Williams, Surveyor, Texas Ranger, and Aunt Ruthie's nephew

Xavier: fictitious old man and neighbor of Molly, flees from Santa Anna with his Anglo American daughter-in-law, Maudie, toddler grandson, and other refugees, and then re-emerges in the story when he returns to Gonzales

Zsohar, Padre: fictitious representation of Zophar from the *Book of Job*, encounters Molly in Matagorda

TRILOGY PLACES

Alabama Trace: no longer exists, located in southeast Texas, it was a native trail west-east connecting Fort Teran to Louisiana

Atascosito: west-east bound road connecting San Antonio, San Felipe, Liberty and Louisiana, roughly the route of present day Highway 10

Bevil: Texan settlement south of Fort Teran and located at the mouth of the Angelina River, presently submerged as a result of water conservation

Camino Real: southwest-northeast bound road connecting Mexico to Laredo, San Antonio, Nacogdoches, and Louisiana

Coushatta Trace: exists only in part today, originally located in southeast Texas, a native trail used by the Coushatta Indians to trade with Mexico, north-south bound, it connected the Sabine River to Bevil, Fort Teran, and Nacogdoches, then extended westward to become the La Bahia Road

Fort Casey: fictitious center of Indian Affairs located near Nacogdoches

Fort Teran: no longer exists, originally established to stop slave smugglers, built by General Terán from Mexico during his inspection of Texas in 1828, located along the Kisatchie Wold on the Neches River; it is also the shallow rock bottom fording place for the Orcoquisac Trace, Coushatta Trace, and the Alabama Trace, and was frequently used by Native Americans, traders, and smugglers

Gotier Trace: (Gōčhər Trace) trail north-south, connecting San Felipe with Matagorda

Harrisburg: destroyed by Santa Anna and becomes present day site of Houston Texas

Harrisburg Road: east-west bound road connecting San Felipe, Harrisburg, Lynchburg, and Liberty

Kisatchie Wold: ridge extending from the Mississippi floodplain to the Rio Grande valley and running roughly east and west and parallel to the Gulf of Mexico, it slopes gradually northward up to 400-450 feet above sea level and then drops off sharply, deflecting rivers, including the Neches River, eastward along its northern edge

La Bahia: road connecting Mexico north-south to Victoria, Goliad, then crossing the Atascosito Road and connecting to Washington-on-the-Brazos, Cole's Settlement, and then northeast to Nacogdoches

La Calle del Norte: road north out of Nacogdoches

La Casa Piedra: commercial building built in 1779 of quarried iron ore stone, including a two-story covered porch, and two stone chimneys, located in Nacogdoches

Neches River: east Texas river which flows generally south to the Gulf of Mexico, deflected east at Kisatchie Wold, which becomes the location of Fort Teran, especially the fording place where multiple native trails merge together, used by smugglers during the 1800s

Orcoquisac Trace: no longer exists, formerly a native trail north-south connecting Liberty to Fort Teran

Trinidad River: renamed Trinity River

Tuck's Landing: fictitious ferryboat crossing along the Atascosito Road at the Trinidad (Trinity) River

Two Mountains: fictitious Comanche village located on the Brazos River in northwest Texas, present day location is called Double Mountain

TRILOGY WORDS AND PHRASES

alcalde: the mayor of a community (Spanish)

acetate of lead: also called sugar lead, causes lead poisoning, a neurotoxin formerly used in the 1700s and 1800s as a sweetener, a fixative for dye, and as a treatment for cholera

bear oil: rendered from bear fat, preferred by Texas settlers in the 1800s as a shortening, binder, or additive in the preparation of breads and pastries

bismuth: since the late 1700s this brittle elemental metal, 86% dense as lead and resembling arsenic, but with low toxicity, is commonly used in colloidal subsalicylate form to treat nausea, heartburn, indigestion, upset stomach, and diarrhea

Brown Bess: surplus Napoleonic muzzle-loading rifle used by the Mexican army during the invasion of Texas by Santa Anna

buckboard: four-wheeled carriage with one or more seats and plank floorboards for cargo

calomel: mercurous chloride, a cathartic used widely from the 1700s until the 1900s, and commonly believed to expel infection from the body by inducing diarrhea

carryall: 1800s slang for a simple carriage, lightweight, four-seats with or without a top, and capable of being drawn by a single horse

catarrh: inflammation of the nose and throat

cholera: plague-like outbreaks of this disease occurred world-wide until 1855 when a bacterium was isolated and discovered to be transmitted through contaminated water, infecting the small intestine, causing profuse diarrhea and vomiting of fishy smelling fluid frequently referred to as rice water, causing rapid loss of bodily fluid, severe dehydration, wrinkled bluish-gray skin, and usually but not always resulting in death

collywobbles: intestinal disorder, bellyache, also 1800s slang for cholera

coneflower: Echinacea

dogtrot: unique Texas building design joining together two cabins in close proximity with a common roof, porch and breezeway

dyspepsia: indigestion

escopeta: muzzle-loading shotgun (Spanish)

exfluncticate: 1800s slang which means to utterly destroy

freebooter: 1800s slang referring to a smuggler

grippe: influenza

hames: part of a harness, a two piece device which encircles a horse's neck for the attachment of reins

laudanum: tincture of opium used as 1800s treatment for various ailments

Mystic Clan: historic criminal organization founded by John A. Murrell

Paterson: first mass produced revolving pistol produced by Samuel Colt in Paterson New Jersey 1836

poultice: cataplasm made of heated cloth and saturated with various types and mixtures of medication and applied to inflamed area of body

pull foot: 1800s slang to leave in a hurry

repeater: see Paterson

rice water: see cholera

root hog or die: 1800s slang meaning to run for your life

sarsaparilla: popular, 1800s beverage similar to root beer, made from the root of the Sassafras albidum

sin-ta-Crockett: 1800s slang, which means behavior causing shame to Davy Crockett

sockdolager: 1800s slang for a sluggard or brawler

sugar lead: see acetate of lead

tasso: dried meat without salt, preservatives, or flavor

Vesuvian: early version of a common stick match

Wapato: edible aquatic plant, Sagittaria, also called Arrowhead

whooping cough: also called pertussis, typically occurring with infants and toddlers; the first stage is mild coughing; the catarrhal stage includes coughing fits followed by a high-pitch sound, vomiting, subconjunctival hemorrhage, fractured ribs, hernia, vertebral artery dissection, and unconsciousness; the paroxysmal stage includes spasms and seizures; usually not fatal when proper care and treatment is administered

TRILOGY ACKNOWLEDGEMENTS

To my lovely wife, Marilyn, I couldn't ask for a better partner. You are the love of my youth, the love of my life, my soul mate, and my best friend. I don't think anyone could write a story about a soul mate, unless they actually have one. While I poured through mountains of treatises, historical writings, diaries, and letters to gather information for the story, you were the only one who believed I could do it. You never stopped encouraging me. But that wasn't all, you also sat patiently for hours, listening to me read and re-read my rough manuscript to you. Your comments and insights helped bring my characters to life, and helped me find my voice. I couldn't have done it without you.

To my favorite daughter-in-law, Deborah, (my only daughter-in-law) I never would have known how much I needed your help if you hadn't come over to listen to my long, long, reading sessions. I wouldn't have gotten any of those Spanish phrases right, and I would have flubbed some of the most important elements in the story. Your inner beauty has spilled over onto my pages. My readers and I are enriched because of it. Your input has been invaluable.

To my father, I solemnly declare to you my dependence. It is my deepest desire to live at the center of your will, doing that which you've laid before me, and fulfilling your purpose. You've provided for the needs of my family, and have kept us safe. Thank You. You've inspired words which please you. I've never been so thrilled to go to work, as I have since you've given me the honor of working in collaboration with you. I will love you and serve you with all my heart and with all my soul, all the days of my life, and then I will be satisfied.

To the Romance Writers of America, thanks, it's been almost twenty years, and I wasn't a member for very long, but the skills you gave me influence my writing today. Not only did I learn how to create mystery, and hook the reader, but I also gained an understanding of romance. Simply stated, romance is life. The story of everyone's life includes romance, more or less. Without it there is usually no story to tell, at least, no meaningful story that folks want to read. So, thanks again, Romance Writers of American. You brought my historical fiction to life by teaching me how to wrap it around an intriguing romance.

This work is lovingly dedicated to my children Matthew and Angela, and their families.

FORWARD TO THE BLACK DRESS TRILOGY

The ***Runaway and Scrapes*** occurred during the Texas Revolution in 1836. The Runaway represents the flight of Texan refugees from Santa Anna and his advancing army to the safety of the United States. The Scrapes represent military skirmishes, which occurred during the war. The Runaway might be the most dramatic, and the most overlooked disaster in American history. To put the event into perspective, imagine that an army invaded America today, and that army had the same proportion to our modern population as Santa Anna had to Texas in 1836. The army in this scenario would number about 70 million. We wouldn't have much of a chance, would we? Those are the odds the Texans faced.

Add genocide to my scenario. If an army of 70 million experienced, high tech soldiers swept across America today, killing everyone, men and women, young and old, destroying every city, and burning every home, we would be wiped off the face of the earth, even if we made a stand against them. The world would be appalled. Is it any wonder that the settlers in 1836 Texas ran for their lives? Shouldn't we be appalled? This tragedy could be the worst disaster ever seen on American soil. That is why I am telling the story of the Runaway.

The loss of life during the Runaway dwarfed the combined losses at the Alamo and Goliad, but the full extent will never be known. While General Houston and the fledgling Republic of Texas were keeping records of their skirmishes (Scrapes) with Santa Anna and his troops, the settlers in the Runaway were not keeping records, except for a few letters and diary entries, which exist today. The refugees were mostly women, children, and the infirm. Taken by surprise, they fled with little or no provisions for the cold, wet, and unsanitary conditions they would face. Criminals found them to be easy prey. As a result, many refugees died along the way to Louisiana. They were buried where they fell, beside the roads they had been traveling on. Using the stories written by those who survived, I've tried to portray what it was like to be a settler, running for their life. From these meager beginnings arose some of the fiercest fighters the world has ever seen, the Texas Rangers.

The Rangers began to emerge before Santa Anna invaded Texas. He'd withdrawn his support from the frontier. Outposts, which were designed to protect the frontier from incursion and depredation, were abandoned. Mexican troops were called away, and the frontier was left defenseless. This was the first sign Santa Anna gave that he wanted Americans to leave Texas. For their own protection the settlers were forced to band together, and from those first defenders emerged the Texas Rangers. The conclusion of the revolution established a need for a standing army to defend the Republic, and like state policemen on steroids, the Rangers filled that need. To this very day they continue to protect Texas. Their story cannot be told without including the story of the first mass produced revolver.

The balance of power had to change or the Republic of Texas would not be able to stand on its own. Fearing that the United States intended to annex Texas, Santa Anna had attempted to drive all the American settlers out. Mexican traders and landowners in Texas aligned themselves with him, and supported his military ambition. Native American tribes viewed Santa Anna's invasion as an opportunity to claim territory from the settlers for themselves. Their interest in Texas can be seen in negotiations they had with Mexico as early as the 1820s. At best the balance of power was about equal between three main struggling forces, American settlers, Mexicans, and natives. Throw in the freebooters and boarder ruffians, who sought refuge from the reach of United States law, include the depredations committed by raiding parties, and the sovereignty of the Republic became precarious. That is, until Samuel Colt invented a five shot repeating pistol called the Paterson.

One of the difficulties with defending the Republic was the weapons they used. A muzzle-loading rifle could not be fired from horseback because of its large size and weight. Prior to the introduction of the Paterson revolver, the Rangers responded to depredations by first pursuing their enemies, and then dismounting to fire their muzzle-loaders. They only had one shot, and it took too long to reload. A mounted Native American could shoot up to twelve arrows point-blank into a Ranger before he could reload his rifle. If the Ranger's enemies were numerous, his chances of success were greatly diminished. When the Paterson revolvers were introduced, the Rangers could ride into a skirmish with two revolvers each, firing ten shots while mounted atop their horses, and they could reload without dismounting. The balance of power changed at that point in favor of the Republic, and that is the point where Molly McCracken's story begins.

Early writings have revealed that many Native Americans coexisted with Texan settlers before the revolution. Only a few tribes were aggressive, and those were also the largest tribes. What I've seen in those writings was not the stereotypical Native American, as seen on television or in the movies. I've attempted to express this truth in my writing. Granted, their attire and their behavior differed from that of the settlers, but that's what makes the story colorful and interesting. I will show things about Native American life, which the reader has never seen in word before. Molly McCracken's trouble is caused by the life and times of 1836 Texas, rather than Native American depredations. Her troubles grieve her, and like Job, her troubles arouse within her an age old question.

Volumes have been written about Job. I've read some of them, and I've read the *Book of Job* several times. It explores life's most difficult questions. Those who survived the Runaway were probably asking themselves those same questions. When I noticed the similarity between Job and Molly McCracken, I decided to winnow the book down to its essence, and include the essence in Molly's story.

First, I searched for period names, which sounded like the names of Job's accusers. Eliphaz became Pastor Eli Phipps, Bildad became

Christiana Biladeau, Zophar became Padre Zsohar, and Elihu became Elli-Lou Susser.

Pastor Phipps quotes Eliphaz to condemn Molly and the refugees traveling with her. He believes they are wicked and have been punished and driven out of their homes due to their wickedness. He tells them that if they confess their wickedness they will be restored.

Christiana Biladeau is more interested in her views about suffering than she is in the actual suffering of those around her. She accuses Molly of complaining, believing that she should rather be examining her relationship with her Creator.

Padre Zsohar's opinions not only condemn Molly, but they express the general feelings of period Hispanics toward the Americano. Suggesting that God will extract restitution from all Americanos, he implies that restitution will also be extracted from Molly. She will have to pay for her wickedness. Since Catholicism was the official religion of Mexico at that time, and was imposed on Texas, I've portrayed Molly as a Catholic.

Elli-Lou Susser accuses Molly of questioning the character of the Almighty. She believes that Molly should accept her trouble, and search for what the Almighty wants her to learn from it.

Elli-Lou's husband, Franklin, offers a dissertation on why the innocent suffer, based on his battlefield experience when he was visited by the archangel Uriel.

Angelology isn't included in literature much anymore, and a story about Catholicism in Texas probably shouldn't exclude Angelology. It's part of the biblical canon. The archangels of the four winds were Gabriel, Michael, Raphael, and Uriel. The reader might not have heard of Uriel. That's because a tendency to worship angels caused Uriel to be removed from the Church's veneration in AD 745. Some have portrayed Uriel as the angel of death. I found this portrayal particularly intriguing, because in south Texas there exists among some Catholics a tradition of venerating a being they call Santo Muerte, the Saint of Death. It is rumored that Santo Muerte is actually worshiped in some places. Is it possible that Santo Muerte is Uriel? Molly McCracken's story explores this possibility.

PREFACE TO THE BLACK DRESS TRILOGY

Black Dress is historical fiction, which is a contrived story set in historical fact. Though I've identified this story as fiction, the reader needs to understand that it connects together all the bits of truth and historical reality I could weave in. There is no other way to tell the story of the Runaway. Not enough is known. I've tried to make it an interesting read, and as accurate as possible, but I expect to get comments about the story not being right or not happening a certain way. That's why I've identified it as fiction. Others might complain about the way I write dialogue, because folks didn't talk in 1836 south Texas the way I wrote dialogue. I've read period lingua franca, and most readers wouldn't tolerate it.

Molly McCracken is a fictitious character. Her story is inspired by accounts of depredations, which occurred prior and during the invasion of Texas by Santa Anna. She flees from Gonzales before it is burned in 1836. The town folks, their farms, and the mercantile are also fictitious. Their names and hers are not intended to imply or resemble any historical persons.

The scouts, soldiers, and General Houston's arrival at Molly McCracken's camp is fictitious. Though we know that something similar actually occurred, the explanation Houston offers to the town folks concerning his abandonment of the Alamo and retreat from Gonzales is also fictitious. Though I've tried to create a scene as historically accurate as possible, the exact events and words spoken will never be known. Based on my studies of Houston's character and accomplishments, I've written what I thought he might have said, and how I thought the town folks would have responded.

Molly's flight from Santa Anna is based on my own inspection of the approximate route taken during the Runaway. Conditions and incidents along the way are taken directly from the accounts of those who survived, and are embellished to fit her story.

Molly arrives in San Felipe before it is burned. I've attempted to describe period building construction as accurately as possible, but I've embellished the layout of the settlement to fit the story.

Molly visits Missis Powell's Tavern before it is burned by General Urrea. I don't know what the establishment looked like, and little is known about Missis Powell. I created buildings which fit the period. In this story Missis Powell is a fictitious character. She is real in name only. I gave her an appearance, personality, and words, which fit both history and the story.

The next settlement Molly visits is Matagorda. I created what I thought a small, industrial seaport would look like in 1836. The characters who occur there, and those from there, are fictitious, and are not intended to resemble anyone.

Buffalo Head and his gang of Comancheros are fictitious, but their crimes are based on actual historical accounts.

The thicket along Gotier Trace is fictitious, and is inspired by my own experience in the Big Thicket.

The cabin on Gotier Trace and the Rangers using it are fictitious, but created for the story to be similar to historical accounts. Captain Boots Williams is a combination of several noteworthy Texas Rangers, and is not intended to resemble anyone in particular.

Tuck's Landing is fictitious. Though it reflects period construction, it is not intended to resemble anything in history. The characters at Tuck's Landing are fictitious. The owner, the owner's family and all relatives are fictitious. Their names are not intended to resemble anyone from that or any period.

The settlement of Liberty is real, but my description is fictitious. The festival, the town folks, and the businesses are also fictitious.

Fort Teran was real, no longer exists, and is embellished to fit the story. Sam Pallet is fictitious. His appearance, the things he says, and any implications the reader might derive concerning him are fictitious. His character was created to fit the story.

John Murrell was a real criminal, and the Mystic Clan was a real criminal organization. I've tried to incorporate historical facts concerning him and his clan into the story. His appearance is derived from historical accounts. Nomusha, Hamadi, and Adama are fictitious victims of the mystic clan. Their story is inspired by crimes, which Murrell actually committed.

The appearance and behavior of Native American tribes residing in Texas in 1836 are derived from period descriptions, and embellished to fit the story. Incidents involving Native Americans, which occur in the story, are also taken directly from those same descriptions and embellished.

The reader should find Nacogdoches an interesting place to visit in word. My book club liked Nacogdoches so much they wanted the main characters to return and make it their home. The businesses and business owners, as described, are fictitious. Their names are not intended to resemble anyone. La Casa Piedra is real, and I've tried to include it accurately in the story. Vicente Córdova and Juan Mora are real historical characters in name only. Their physical description, mannerisms, and the words they say are fictitious, but are intended to reflect what I think they might have said and done.

The Owen farm and characters are fictitious, and are not intended to resemble anyone or anything.

Fort Casey, Colonel Martin Casey, and the Rangers at Fort Casey are fictitious and are not intended to resemble anyplace or anyone, but are inspired by period events.

The Cherokee village and the Comanche village are fictitious villages set in real places. I've tried to depict living conditions, behavior, and attire as accurately as possible based on period accounts.

The depictions of the hostel and infirmary in San Antonio are fictitious. Doctor Arnwine is fictitious. Colonel Karnes and R. C. Timble are real historical characters, but their role in the story is fictitious. The things they are supposed to have said were created to fit the story.

The infirmary in Lynchburg is fictitious.

Plantations owned by Milliken, and owned by LaMonte are fictitious. Their names are not intended to resemble anyone.

RUNAWAY FEVER

Black Dress Trilogy Volume 1

PROLOGUE: THE ATTIC

AFTER GRANDMA DIED, Mom wanted to divide her belongings among Grandma's children and grandchildren, so I volunteered to help her sort and pack Grandma's things. On Saturday, my wife and I rented a moving van, picked Mom up at her house, and drove down to Grandma's tiny bungalow in Gonzales.

We spent the morning loading household items and furniture. Most of it would be donated to the needy. At first Mom was gloomy, but after a few hours packing up Grandma's belongings, she found closure in her labor, and said goodbye to her mom. In Grandma's bedroom we found jewelry, but none of it was real. After lunch we packed the kitchen. Later in the afternoon we cleaned out the pantry.

Opening the pantry door reminded me of those comedy shows where stuff in the closet collapses when the door is opened. Well, it didn't collapse, but we spent over an hour sorting and packing piles of old table service, small appliances, which didn't work, and countless boxes of both dry and canned goods, some over ten years old. I'd forgotten that there was a small door in the back of the pantry. Then I remembered it from my childhood. It opened to a narrow stairway, which led up to a low attic. I used to believe it was a passageway to hidden treasure, and that's exactly what it turned out to be, as we were about to discover.

For the first time since I was a child my feet entered the attic. Walking hunched over on the creaky boards, we stirred up ages of dust, speckling the sunbeams, which spilled from a small window from one end of the attic to the other. Boxes were stacked at the far end. In them we found additional house wares, kitchenware, old clothing, and Christmas decorations. When we removed the last of the boxes, we found behind them a very old trunk shoved against the slope of the roof. It had a rounded top, was made of oak, and had darkened black with age. The leather straps and handles had rotted away, leaving black stubs poking out through the sides. The lock was broken, and the front had a hole in it about the size of my thumb.

At that point our imaginations ran away on what we knew about outlaws and Indians; after all, we lived in Texas. Mom remembered the trunk from when she was growing up. She was allowed to look inside, but not allowed to touch anything or take anything out. Grandma told her that it had been passed down from her mom, and it had belonged to her mom's great grandmother, who settled with her family in Gonzales back in the eighteen hundreds. Burning with curiosity, I had to open it and see what was inside.

The musty smell of old things wafted up in our faces, as three of us knelt before the trunk, and opened the lid. We found personal items, very old items, like a hair brush with bent over bristles. Mom said the bristles were made from hog's hair. There were a lot of little bottles with nothing in them. I picked up a hand mirror with a piece of antler for a handle, and found the reflective surface had corrupted. A rusty old dagger with a cracked and yellowed ivory handle was pretty cool. And, there was a small wooden box, possibly a jewelry box. It had been made by a craftsman, for it was dovetailed at the corners and nailed shut with tiny nails. Grandma knew what was inside, but never let anyone open it. Mom believed it was a secret stash of money, so she pulled the top off. I had to laugh, because the only things inside were an old Lone Ranger mask, which could be held up on a stick, and a small porcelain doll, a toy doll small enough for a child to swallow. Returning the items to the box, she fitted the nails into their holes, and pressed the lid back into place.

Beneath the personal items lay a quilt, folded and yellow with age. Below that, we found several crude-looking dresses made of brittle fabric. I tried to unfold them, so we could have a look, but the fabric began to break at the creases when I opened them. Mom stopped me, and explained that Grandma had told her that the clothing was made by our ancestors. The garments didn't seem so crude when I realized they were family heirlooms. Setting them carefully aside, I noticed that one had been dyed black, for the seams of the dress revealed an underlying lavender color.

Beneath the clothing, at the bottom of the trunk I found several bundles, wrapped with leather, and tied with brittle laces. Two of the bundles were oblong and quite heavy. I picked up one of them and tried to open it. The leather crumbled in my hands, and an old pistol rolled out, a strange looking revolver. The butt stock was broken, with what looked like a lead ball imbedded in it. Inscribed on the frame was the word Paterson. I hadn't seen anything like it before. It was caked with dried grease, and looked like a valuable antique, and there appeared to be another one like it.

A larger bundle was completely black, and surprisingly light. Harder and more brittle than the other bundles, it was also made of leather. I peeled the edges back to look inside and found something really odd. It looked like a tightly packed ball of potato chips with hair on them.

Mom stopped me from opening it any further. She'd found a diary and wanted to look it over before opening anything else. The cover of the diary broke away from its binding when she opened it. I could tell that she felt bad about breaking the cover. Seating herself on a wooden crate, she carefully turned the brittle pages, and skipped over several entries. My wife and I found a couple of ragged folding chairs, brushed them off, and seated ourselves.

Mom began to read the diary to us, and said, "'March 13, 1836. We've just been informed that the Alamo has fallen. Santa Anna has executed one hundred and eighty nine of our beloved defenders. Thirty of them were from Gonzales, and I fear that my husband, Emmet, has been among them. Riders came through today and warned us of the massacre. They said that Santa Anna has ten thousand soldiers marching against Gonzales, and they are a mere two hours away. They are armed with rifle, sword and cannon, and they have set their intentions upon driving us out of Texas. They will show us no mercy. They will butcher men, women, and youngsters, as they have butchered our brave defenders at the Alamo. They will burn to the ground our farms and our towns, leaving nothing for us to return to, should we escape. We had not time to make provision for our departure.

Everyone, including myself, has been taken with runaway fever, and we have left our homes in great haste.'"

RUNAWAY FEVER

MOLLY MCCRACKEN COULDN'T see who it was. Horses had been clopping up the road all night, and in the darkness of a moonless, starless night the horses all sounded the same. Concluding her diary entry by firelight, she blew the ink dry, and closed the cover on the worst day of her life. Her husband was dead. She, her sister, her little niece, and the entire town of Gonzales were running for their lives. Her heart wouldn't stop fluttering, and her tears came in uncontrollable bursts. Wrapping her diary in a patch of leather, she nervously tied it, climbed up into their farm wagon, and tucked it into the family sea-chest.

The clopping Molly heard pulled up by the campfire. To her relief it was Innis, her brother-in-law. Hastily he dismounted and ran to Molly's sister, Emily, his wife, who threw her arms around him, and cried, "I was afraid you had been killed."

"I came as soon as I heard," Innis explained. "I came to take you some place safe. Then I'll go back."

"You're going back?"

"We can't let them kick us off our land," he insisted. Turning to Molly, he said, "I need to talk to you about Emmet."

"You're going to tell me he's dead, aren't you?"

"There's things you don't know yet, Molly. Things he didn't want to tell you."

Climbing down from the wagon, Molly warmed herself by the fire, as Emily pulled Innis over to a skillet of salt-pork, sizzling on a bed of coals. "Sit here," she urged him. "Let me get you something to eat, and you can tell us everything that happened."

"Where's Amy?" he asked.

"She's asleep in the wagon."

Tendrils of bacon-like smoke filled the air, as Innis sat cross-legged by the campfire, and took a deep breath. From the sea-chest Emily fetched a tin plate, spooned up a serving of salt pork, and added a helping of steamy cornbread from another pan. Presenting to him the plate, she said, "Now tell us what happened at the Alamo. It must have been horrible."

"Let me eat first," he replied, and proceeded to devour his meal.

Spooning another helping onto his plate, Emily asked, "You haven't eaten today, have you?"

"Been two days," he mumbled.

"Doesn't the army feed you?"

"Not exactly. It's every man for himself. Everyone carries their own food."

"I don't understand," Emily continued. "I've heard that the Alamo was well supplied."

Chewing, as he watched Emily, he did not respond, and Molly thought it odd that he wouldn't answer such a simple question. Normally, he was a fountain of information. Then Molly added, "That's what I heard, too. I heard the Alamo was stocked up for a siege."

"That's right," Innis finally replied.

Lifting her palms, Emily shrugged and asked, "Then why do you have to carry your own food?"

Again he did not answer.

Emily persisted. "I'm glad that some of you could get away from the Alamo. How did you get away?"

"Everyone at the Alamo was killed," he said. "Nobody got away. I didn't get away, because I wasn't there." Rocking back on his elbows, he kicked his feet out in front of him, and crossed his ankles.

Molly's heart leapt with joy, and she clasped her hands together. "If you weren't there, then that means Emmet wasn't there either. That means he wasn't killed at the Alamo? Is he still alive?"

Her sister, Emily, knelt to embrace her husband, and said, "I'm glad you weren't there, Innis. I'm glad y'all weren't killed with the others, but I don't understand."

"Did y'all see that?" someone yelled from the darkness behind them.

Turning his head, Innis hollered, "Who's there?"

"It's me. It's Henry Hort." Out of the shadows an elderly man stepped, halting and bent, and spitting mosquitoes. Beneath his bushy white beard he seemed somber, as he said, "Did y'all see them flashes over yonder?"

Lifting her eyes to the western horizon, Molly noticed the flashes right away, and also saw traces of bright orange along the edges of distant storm clouds, like sunset, though it was far past sunset. Moments later, rumblings shook the air. "I think there's a storm coming," she speculated. "And, we don't have any shelter tonight."

"It's not a thunderstorm," Innis contended.

Peering into the darkness behind her, Molly could yet see campfires flickering through a stand of shadow-laden Post oak, the campfires of the town folks who had fled with her and Emily throughout the night. From the trees echoed yet the puling and wailing of women and youngsters, wives and mothers, who grieved the loss of their loved ones at the Alamo.

"Is that you Innis Carrigan?" Henry Hort lifted his bushy white eyebrows. "Sakes alive, I didn't know y'all was here with us? Didn't I see you leave with the other boys on their way to the Alamo? I thought you went with them to join the fight."

"I just rode in," Innis replied. "I come back to get my family to someplace safe."

Slapping the back of his neck, and then scratching, Henry Hort asked, "Y'all came back from the Alamo? How'd you do that? I heard everyone there was killed." Henry pointed toward the western horizon, and said, "There's them flashes again. There's a storm a coming."

"It's a storm alright," Innis agreed. "But, it ain't a thunder storm. There's a fight going on back in Gonzales. It looks to me like the whole town's on fire. That glow rising up on those clouds yonder is a big old fire, and that's right about where Gonzales would be. That thunder you're hearing ain't thunder. It's cannon."

Prickles rose on the back of Molly's neck. Bolting around to gaze again at the glow on the horizon, the truth became obvious to her. Gonzales was burning. That meant her homestead was burning, and next door, Emily's homestead was burning also.

Emily dropped her face into her hands, and whimpered, "That means we've lost everything. What will we do now? Where will we go? We have nowhere to go."

Reaching around Emily's shoulders, Molly held her sister tight, and said, "We're here, aren't we? We're not there, thank goodness."

From Emily, Molly's gaze fell into the campfire, and into the skillet, where it sizzled for a moment with the salt pork. As she watched the skillet, the wind picked up and blew white-hot the coals underneath, lifting embers into the darkness. Drifting up through bare tree branches, the embers rose into a black sky, where they burned out. They also drifted over into the winter-dead grass beyond the campfire and flared into raging flames. In those flames Molly imagined her house blazing up, and imagined Emily's house blazing up next to hers, as Innis and Henry jumped into the flames.

Like demons dancing in hell, Innis and Henry commenced stomping out the grassfire, much as Santa Anna's cannon had commenced stomping out their homes in Gonzales, sending a firestorm of white-hot embers into the sky. Molly could yet hear the rumblings from Gonzales, could feel them in the air around her.

Tightening her embrace on Emily, Molly led her sister away from the flames. Fire was no friend of a woman's cotton dress. Shaking her head, she whispered to Emily, "I don't know where we'll go from here."

"Maybe we should go back to New Orleans," Emily suggested.

Innis spun around to face his wife. The grassfire was out, but flared yet in his dark blue eyes. "Balderdash," he grumbled. "We ain't going back to New Orleans. I'm taking you someplace safe for now, and when the fight is over, we'll rebuild our homesteads and barns, and plow our fields again. This is where we put our roots down, Emily, right here in Texas, just like we all agreed before we came here. Remember when we agreed to come here and put down our roots?"

"I remember," Emily acceded.

"You said you liked it here," Innis continued.

Emily nodded. "I like it here just fine."

Stomping the charred grass, Innis flailed his arms and kicked his feet a little more than necessary, even though the fire was out.

"Just leave him be," Molly suggested, and pulled Emily back another step further away from him. "He's angry. Can't you see he's angry?"

"Yes."

Behind them, in the darkness, brush snapped and crunched. Molly turned to look for another flare up, but realized that what she heard was town folks crashing through the brush toward her.

"Well Innis," Henry exclaimed, as he put his foot down on an ember. "I'm glad y'all are here. You're the most able bodied man amongst us. I think we should post a watch tonight. This here is dangerous country for women-folk and youngins. The Injuns don't want us here, and the Comancheros will pick us clean if we give them a chance."

Spry youngsters emerged first from the brush into the light of the camp-fire, and began stomping on any embers they could find. Puffy eyed women, who were blotting yet their mournful tears, came next. Then Xavier and Uncle Elmer emerged, both men older than Henry. They were followed by the Schaubles, an elderly couple, who had owned the mercantile in Gonzales. All came to help put out the grassfire. Even Maria Benson waddled in, nine months pregnant, and swiping tears from her puffy eyes. Dashing past her into the woods, her five boys searched for any stray embers they might stomp on.

"Ven aquí!" Maria yelled to her boys. "There is no fire in the woods. You can play tomorrow."

To her side they scampered back.

"All right then," Henry addressed them all. "The fire is out. We can't be having a grassfire, and we can't stand around all night flapping our jaw bones about it neither. It's too dangerous here. We need to post a watch, and keep everyone safe, so y'all can get some rest."

Everyone agreed.

"How many rifles we got amongst us?"

One of the boys began to weep, and said, "My pa took our rifle with him to the Alamo, and ma said he ain't a coming back."

Maria Benson's oldest replied, "My pa give me a squirrel rifle," and he held it up for everyone to see.

Leaning on his walking stick, Xavier explained, "I give my rifle to my son. He need very many rifles to take to fight at the Alamo. Now, I do not have rifle."

"I got mine here." Henry stood his rifle butt against the ground, and clasped his hand around the barrel. "That's two rifles amongst us. We'll have to take turns with them."

Innis indicated the rifle scabbard attached to the saddle on his horse, and said, "I have one."

"All right then. That's three rifles. Good. So, me, Innis, and one of you boys can take first watch."

With his rifle in hand, Innis slipped silently out among the trees. Henry slung his rifle over his arm and walked into the darkness, halting and bent, crunching twigs and brush beneath his feet. Maria's oldest took his squirrel rifle in a direction opposite from Henry. Then the blackest of nights began to shed a cold spring mist upon them all.

From the north the wind stiffened, howling through the bare Post oak. Cold drizzle and falling temperatures drove the town folks to their camps. A chill sank into Molly's bones. Crossing her arms, she rubbed them with her hands, and said, "I knew it was going to rain. At least it's driving the mosquitoes away. I'll get our cloaks." Climbing into the wagon, she put on her cloak and glanced down at her little niece Amy who had curled up under a quilt between the sea-chest and the sideboard, atop a sack of parched corn. "Amy is getting wet and cold back here," she told Emily.

Climbing in with Molly, Emily said, "I'll take her." Lifting the towheaded three-year-old from the damp quilt that covered her, Emily added, "We can sleep under the wagon tonight. I don't know what else to do."

"Mommy?" the toddler asked.

"It's all right, baby." Wrapping Amy papoose style in a dry blanket from the sea-chest, Emily left a flap that would cover her face.

Molly could remember yet the moment Amy was born, the first breath she drew, and the first sound she made. Recalling the contentment on Emily's face, she also recalled her longing to have her own children, but couldn't love Amy any more, even if she had been her own. As Amy's deep blue, smiling eyes peeked up at Molly from inside the wooly cocoon, Molly said, "I love you, Amy."

"Lub you, Aunt Lolly," the three-year-old replied.

"Did you see my cloak?" Emily asked.

"No. Did you put it in the sea-chest?"

"I don't remember."

Searching the chest, Molly could not find Emily's cloak. She pulled off her own cloak, and offered it to Emily, saying, "Here, take mine. You and Amy need it more than I do."

"But, you'll freeze," Emily protested.

"I'll wrap up in one of these quilts. I'll be fine."

"Hold up there!" a gruff voice shouted through the trees.

Molly could see nothing in the misty darkness.

"Who are you?" The voice from the trees shouted again, and sounded like Henry Hort about forty or fifty paces out. "Better stop right where you are or I'll shoot."

"Don't shoot. Don't shoot," someone answered. "We got but one rifle, and we got no ball for it. We are unarmed."

"There's more than just you?"

"Yes, sir. There's five of us. We're scouting for General Houston."

"That so? Where you boys coming from then?"

"Gonzales, sir. We're running from Santa Anna, running like old Redbones with our tails tucked twixt our legs. General Houston's orders. He's coming too, right behind us with a couple hundred reinforcements. He's afraid to fight, sir, and he's a darn drunk too. I seen him drinking soon as he gets up in the morning. If y'all ask me, he's a coward and ain't fit to command no army."

"All right then. You boys come on in."

Wrapping herself in a quilt, Molly climbed down from the wagon and watched the scouts ride in. Some of the town folks returned to watch them pull up at her dwindling campfire, and dismount.

"Have y'all heard from Emmet?" someone asked behind Molly.

Glancing back, Molly recognized the tiny strawberry mole under the left eye of her close friend and best neighbor. Reaching out to her, Molly asked, "Elli-Lou Susser? Is that you?" She, Emily, and Elli-Lou used to gather together on spinning day with some of the other neighbors and weave cloth and make clothing for their families. When one was ill, the others pitched in to help with household chores. "How long have you been here?" Molly asked.

"Me and Uncle Elmer pulled in before dark. We were among the first ones in tonight. I saw y'all come in late. Is everything okay? Have you heard from Emmet?"

"I haven't."

"I haven't heard from Franklin either. He's supposed to be with General Houston. Who are these boys who just came in?"

"They say they're scouts for General Houston."

In the light of the campfire the scouts came threadbare and bedraggled. Their shirts and britches were wet and had holes in them. Only one of them had a hat on his head, a hat woven from grass, now soggy and drooping. Another carried the only rifle. Each had a satchel or a sack slung over his shoulder. One had a crop of unruly, dripping red hair, and his face was splattered with freckles. He seemed to lead the others. Molly thought they all looked like farm boys who'd just come in from the fields. "Where's your uniforms?" she asked.

They laughed at her, and the red-haired leader answered, "There ain't no uniforms, ma'am. And, there ain't no rifles, neither. And, there ain't no food, except what we stuffed in our packs. We throwd everything in the fire. Houston's orders."

"Did y'all see Santa Anna?" Molly asked. "Did he attack Gonzales, like everyone said?"

"Yes, ma'am, we saw him from afar when we was scouting."

He and the other scouts seated themselves on the ground next to the fire, and added wood. The red-haired scout turned his attention to a wooden handle that one of the womenfolk placed in his hand, and the tiny smelting pot that was attached to it. He held the tool over the fire to heat a lead ingot she had dropped in, and kept it there until the lead became molten.

Pressing him for more information, Molly asked, "Riders came through Gonzales and said there was ten thousand soldiers coming to attack us. Did you see ten thousand soldiers?"

"Well ma'am, what I seen looked more like chiggers swarming over an ant hill. I think it was more like twenty thousand, maybe thirty thousand."

As the lead in the little smelting pot became molten, he poured the heavy liquid into a borrowed mold, and cast ball for his rifle.

"Did you fight them?" Molly persisted. "We heard cannon. And, we can see the fire from here. Gonzales is burning, isn't it?"

"There weren't no fight, ma'am. Much as we wanted for it. That's why we came here. We wanted to help General Houston fight old Santa Anna. We heard about that letter from Colonel Travis, asking for help at the Alamo, and we decided to pull foot and come fight." He hung his head. "I'm abashed to say it, but General Houston called a retreat before Santa Anna got there. He run from the fight, ma'am. He's a skunk, and he skunked all us. Then he ordered that Gonzales be set afire, and he ordered us to burn everything in our camp we couldn't carry."

"Horses coming!" Henry's voice bellowed through the trees again. "And wagons. I hear wagons."

"That'd be Houston," the red-haired soldier replied.

Molly continued, "I heard cannon. I heard it, and I saw the flashes."

"Yes, ma'am, I heard it too, but them flashes weren't cannon. They was kegs or something going off inside them buildings we set afire."

"And you say General Houston ordered you to set Gonzales on fire? It wasn't Santa Anna?"

"Yes, ma'am."

The womenfolk gasped. Xavier, Uncle Elmer, Titus Schauble, and the younger boys all shook their heads. Missis Schauble began to weep and cried out, "Have mercy. Lordy, have Mercy. It's all for naught."

First to canter in was General Houston, shoulders back, bobbing with his chestnut mare, and leading about a dozen mounted soldiers. His black waistcoat, sword, and knee-high boots made him appear official. Pulling back his reins, the firelight illuminated his clean shaven and cleft chin between his bushy sideburns. Molly knew few men who troubled themselves with shaving. Looking straight at her with grim determination in his dark eyes, she could tell that he wasn't seeing her or anyone in particular, as he said, "I would like to extend to all you folks my sincerest regrets for the loss of your loved ones at the Alamo."

"Y'all abandoned our boys," Mister Titus Schauble hollered at him, and shook his fist.

"You left my husband to be slaughtered by men who are mad," Maria Benson yelled, "Now my boys they do not have a father."

"Yeah!" Henry shouted.

"Yeah!" The others in unison agreed.

The face of the red-haired scout blushed, as he listened and cast another rifle ball.

"Y'all may as well have run our boys through with your own sword," Mister Schauble hollered at him, shaking yet his fist.

"With all due respect, sir," General Houston continued. "Some time ago I perceived what the outcome of our resistance at the Alamo would be. The fortification is weak and inadequate at best. So, I dispatched soldiers to dismantle and abandon the Alamo before Santa Anna and his troops should arrive. It was my intention to move them to a more defensible position. We desperately needed to add those men to our ranks, and we needed their cannon, and their supplies to replenish our forces. We are greatly diminished without them. But, they refused to leave, sir. They refused, and if I had taken our meager reinforcements to defend them against an army of four thousand Mexican regulars, we would have all been defeated, and Santa Anna could then march unopposed through our land."

The town folks became silent.

"We're at war," General Houston continued. "Sacrifices must be made. Our very lives, our republic, and our freedom are at stake. Is there any price that you would not be willing to pay?"

Again, no one answered.

Turning to his men, he barked his orders, "We'll bivouac yonder in that clearing. Set up a perimeter and guard. There's not much time until sunrise so try to get some rest and be prepared to move early." Nudging his horse, he turned toward the clearing.

Behind General Houston the lead soldier was taller in the saddle than the others. His sandy, wavy hair hung almost to the collar of his jacket. Except for him, all the other soldiers wore full beards. Even the youngest among them had a crop of fuzz outlining his jaw. Over their legs they wore chaps. Molly noticed that the scouts who arrived first didn't have chaps on their legs.

These were not ordinary soldiers. Their leather coats were oiled to shed the rain, and underneath their coats they all wore red shirts. Behind their belts she could see knives and pistols. Supply packs were tied to their saddles, and their rifles were protected by oiled leather scabbards with tie down flaps.

As the soldiers entered the clearing, supply wagons clattered in, and other soldiers began to arrive on foot. Those who had tents pitched them as the wind drove the town folks again to their wagons and their wet blankets. No one owned a covered wagon. They were too expensive, and considered unnecessary in Texas, except for tonight.

At Molly's side, Elli-Lou shivered. Molly told her, "I'll stay with you and watch for Franklin." Around both of them Molly draped the quilt she was wearing, and together they huddled, sharing each other's warmth.

The soldiers came in muddy, drenched, and looking about as weary as Molly felt. None of them paused to talk. Those who would answer their questions had neither known nor heard of Emmet McCracken or Franklin Susser. When the last of them had entered the clearing, Molly had no choice but to conclude that neither Emmet nor Franklin were among General Houston's troops.

Pondering where in Texas her husband, Emmet, might be, she also wondered if he was thinking of her. Was he in danger? Was he still alive? Overwhelmed with discouragement, she hugged Elli-Lou and said, "Tomorrow we'll talk some more, okay?"

"Okay, Molly. Goodnight."

Under the wagon Molly crawled with Emily and Amy to escape the rain. Emily had knocked down the winter-dead grass by laying a quilt over it, which helped insulate them from the ground. The wind continued to whip a cold mist under the wagon, so Molly cast her quilt over theirs, and sidled next to Emily, pulling the quilts over her head.

"Molly?" Emily whispered. "Are you alright?"

"Yes, but I'm worried about Emmet."

"What are you going to do?"

"I'll try to talk to General Houston tomorrow. Try to find out if he knows where Emmet is. Did Innis tell you anything?"

Innis crawled under the wagon, spread his bedroll over everyone, and slid in next to Emily, opposite Molly. "Houston's posted a guard," he said. "I don't need to stand watch in the rain tonight."

"Innis?" Molly asked, as she pulled the blankets down from her face, and rolled up onto her elbow. "What were you going to tell me about Emmet? You said that you didn't go to the Alamo. Does that mean he's alive?"

"Well, Molly," he sighed. "Now that the whole town ain't listening, I can tell you. Emmet heard that Houston ordered the Alamo abandoned, and he decided he didn't want to go there with the others from Gonzales. He didn't want you or the other folks to think he was a coward either, so we went looking for General Houston. We wanted to sign up with his reinforcements instead. Problem is we couldn't find him. Emmet is still out there looking for him right now. When we heard the Alamo had fallen, we agreed that one of us should come back and get you womenfolk where it's safe. So, we flipped a coin, and it was me. I came to Gonzales and run straight into Houston and his reinforcements. They told me y'all were heading for Louisiana, and from there you know the rest."

Molly rolled onto her back and said, "Then we don't know where he is?"

"Not just yet," Innis replied.

Pulling the blankets again over her head, Molly didn't think she could ever fall asleep under these conditions, especially on the lumpy, hard ground. But, nestled under the blankets with her loved ones, she began to warm up and relax, and listen to the pattering rain on the wagon above her. A day filled with hasty packing and a long, bumpy ride in a wagon began to take its toll. Overtaken by fatigue, she drifted off.

Drifting deeper, she began to dream. She dreamed that she was back in New Orleans. Working together as seamstresses again, she and Emily were on a plantation. Emily was showing her a new twisting stitch that she used for making tatted buttons out of thread.

"Molly McCracken."

Molly thought that she heard her name whispered, like it came from the next room, or maybe through the open window next to her in the mansion, where she was working.

"Molly McCracken."

Again she heard her name, and it stabbed fear into her veins, for she heard it clearly. Her heart pounded her dream into full consciousness, and she opened her eyes. Emily was asleep next to her with Amy, and beyond them Innis snored. Molly drew a deep, sleepy breath, and closed her eyes again. It was a dream, just a bad dream.

"Molly McCracken."

This time she heard it plain, like the wind speaking her name, and she wasn't asleep either. It came from her side of the wagon. Pulling the quilts down from her face, she tried to see who had spoken to her.

THE DREAM

MOLLY MCCRACKEN WONDERED if someone was playing a cruel joke on her. Why would anyone want to whisper her name in the dark, especially during a time of desperate flight from an enemy, such as Santa Anna? Was it her husband, Emmet?

Searching the darkness beyond the smoldering campfire, she could see a light. Looking again, she suspected that it could be the campfire of a neighbor, or maybe, she was seeing a star. The night was overcast and rainy. It couldn't be a star. As she watched, the light grew in intensity. Against it she shielded her eyes, and she began to perceive in the brightness a radiant figure, like a beautiful woman, wearing a flowing white gown, and standing in the midst of the winter-dead grass.

Wind whipped under and over the wagon, heaving up waves of dead grass around the beautiful woman, lifting them like flames, and twirling them around her, as if protecting her, but not consuming her. Away from Molly she'd turned her face, but what Molly could see shone with the brilliance of the sun. Though the wind suddenly died down, the woman's long, black hair and her brilliant white gown rippled into the darkness behind her, like water flowing into the night.

In her arms the woman held a child wrapped in a radiant white blanket, and in her hand she held a cup, which looked like a golden chalice. When she turned her eyes to Molly, her gaze pierced Molly's heart, separated her thoughts from her fears, childhood from adulthood, and past from present and future. Molly gasped, and wanted to turn away, but the woman had power to hold her, as she probed her secrets. Approaching the wagon, the woman knelt and held out to Molly the chalice and with a voice like the wind she said, "Take this cup."

Molly jolted up and knocked her head on the wagon's floorboards, giving herself a wave of dizziness and white flashes. Then onto her back she dropped, rubbing her head with one hand and propping herself with the other. Searching the darkness again, all she could see was darkness, no flames, no brilliant light, and no beautiful woman. The dream had vanished, and the woman was gone.

"What's wrong, Molly?" Emily asked.

"I'm okay, just a nightmare. Go back to sleep." Her heart was practically leaping out of her chest when she lay back, and she doubted if she could ever sleep again. But, the moments passed and the pounding in her chest subsided into a powerful wave of fatigue. Before she realized it, she was a seamstress again in New Orleans.

Twigs snapped and footsteps ran straight at the wagon Molly slept under, startling her awake. Someone shouted. Opening her eyes, and knowing better than to sit up too fast, she noticed that the Post oak around their camp had taken on an eerie green glow. Night had given way to morning drizzle, which leaked between the floorboards, soaking her blankets, and robbing her warmth.

"Houston's moving out!" a soldier shouted, as he ran past the wagon, snapping twigs, and stomping off toward the Schauble camp.

Innis sat up, and struck his head on the floorboards the same way Molly had a few hours before. "Ouch," he hollered. Plopping onto his back, he rubbed his head.

"Houston's moving out," the soldier shouted again, but farther away this time.

Rolling out from under the wagon and into the rain, Innis stood, slapped his hat on his head, and informed them, "I'll get the wagon hitched. You better get yourselves ready."

"Do you think that bump on the head knocked any sense into him?" Emily asked, as she crawled out with Amy into the rain.

"It would take something a lot harder than that," Molly replied.

"I heard that," Innis mumbled as he dropped the kingpin into the wagon's hitch.

Crawling out, Molly climbed up onto the wagon next to Emily and Amy and stood shivering in the wind, her dress slapping against her calves like wet washrags. "I didn't think it was going to be like this," she declared. "I wasn't expecting this cold rain." Against the wind she tightened her bonnet.

"Would you like your cloak back?" Emily asked.

"No. You and Amy keep it," Molly replied.

"Things will get better, Molly. I know they will."

"I'll look for your cloak again," Molly explained. "Maybe I can find it now that its daylight."

Colder and wetter than she'd ever been, Molly climbed over the back-board to search for Emily's cloak. Before leaving their farms in Gonzales they'd thrown everything they could into the wagon: farm tools, cooking ware, a sack of parched corn, a barrel of recently processed salt-pork and a water barrel. Emily didn't want to leave her prized spinning wheel and loom or the family sea-chest for Santa Anna. Working together, the two of them were able to load all the heavy items. Opening the sea-chest, Molly searched again for the cloak.

Beneath the tableware, Emily's dresses were dry along with Molly's own best lavender dress. She loved the lavender dress, because of the white brocade front and lace collar, which Emily had skillfully stitched in place for her. However, she did not find Emily's cloak. Taking out her prized looking glass, Molly noticed that her hazel eyes were red-rimmed and tired and around her bonnet her auburn tresses hung out, dripping with rain.

"Come on, Molly. We have to go," Innis grumbled.

Tucking her tresses into her bonnet, she tossed the mirror in the trunk, and noticed the soggy quilt that Amy had slept in before they put her under the wagon last night. Wringing it out, she draped it around her shoulders, and decided that it would have to do.

Seating herself next to Emily, she shivered. Innis lifted the reins, cracked them against the backs of the horses and yelled, "Haw!" The wagon lurched ahead, and he drove it onto the road, pulling up behind the Schauble's wagon, waiting for the army to escort them up the road.

Other wagons pulled in behind them, piled with supplies and refugees. Some of the refugees were old or infirm. Most were women and youngsters. From the woods Maria Benson, nine months pregnant, rode her horse to the road. Trudging through the mud, her five boys walked alongside. She didn't have a wagon, and didn't carry any belongings. Offering her a ride, the Schaubles helped her up beside them on their seat-board. This pleased Molly, since Maria's baby was due any day. Two of her oldest boys mounted her horse double, and the smaller boys hunkered in the back of the Schauble's wagon under wet blankets.

Plodding up the road on foot, Xavier steadied himself with his walking stick and led his overloaded mule, as his young daughter-in-law carried her toddler, his only grandson. Innis offered them a ride, consolidated his belongings to the front of the wagon, and helped them up.

A frail looking woman trailed behind with her youngsters and two packhorses. Her eyes were red, swollen, and grief stricken. Molly offered her a ride also, which she accepted. After tying the animals to the rear of the wagon, she and her youngsters settled thankfully in with Xavier, his daughter-in-law, and her toddler.

Five mounted soldiers cantered down the line. Their clopping horses splattered mud over the town folks, causing them to duck in their wagons or jump away from the road. Molly recognized the lead rider from the night before, tall in the saddle, wavy, sandy hair, and ghost-blue eyes, which weren't missing anything. The young soldier with the fuzzy jaw rode by last, and tipped his dripping hat to Molly.

"Are you an officer?" Molly asked.

Reining back his horse, he paused, reset his hat, and smiled, saying, "No, ma'am, I am not. That man down yonder." He pointed at the tall rider with the wavy, sandy hair. "The first one down there, he's Captain Boots Williams. I've been riding with him for a couple years now. We're Rangers, Texas Rangers out of San Antonio. At least we was Rangers until he decided he wanted to exfluncticate Santa Anna, and he can do it too."

"I would like to talk to him? Can you get him to come back?"

Twisting around in his saddle, the young soldier hollered down the line, "Captain Williams, woman over here wants to talk!"

Reining his horse around, Captain Williams galloped back up the line, splashing mud over the wagons and examining everyone and everything as he approached. Pulling up beside the Carrigan wagon, he fixed his ghost-blue eyes on Molly, doffed his hat, and said, "Morning, ma'am."

"Sorry to inconvenience you, Mister Captain Williams, but my husband, Emmet McCracken, is missing. I think he might have signed up with General Houston and I wondered if you might have heard of him or know where he is. Emmet McCracken, do you know him?"

"Never heard of him." Captain Williams jerked his horse around, kicked his spurs, and galloped again down the line.

"Forward!" The command came from somewhere up ahead.

"Forward!" the young Ranger with the fuzzy jaw hollered. Then he leaned toward Molly, and said, "Sorry, ma'am. I don't think Captain Williams is lady-broke."

Molly smirked, and asked, "He's brusque."

"Y'all mean is he a brute? Yes, ma'am, he's a brute all right."

One by one the horses heaved the wagons into motion, clattering east toward the Lavaca River. Hooves and wheels churned the rain-soaked road into a slush of ankle deep mud and dung. Molly watched those who didn't have horse or wagon, as they labored on foot along the side of the road with their belongings and youngsters. Some chose to step out of the mud and into the brush, but they fell behind, as weeds and grasses tangled around their feet.

"Come on up," Molly called to them, and as many as would fit in the wagon climbed aboard, seating themselves along the side boards until there was no more room. The added weight drove the wagon's narrow wheels deep into the mud, and increased the burden on the horses.

Into the morning Innis continued to drive the horses until froth appeared on their shoulders and drizzled down their sides in the rain. Molly knew they would not last the day, because of the load they were drawing. Innis climbed down first, and drove the horses, as he walked alongside the wagon in the mud. Molly and Emily left Amy with Xavier, and climbed down the opposite side of the wagon from Innis. Holding the hems of their dresses, they also waded in the mud. Those refugees who were able, both young and old, climbed down to lighten the load.

From the Post oak they emerged onto a plain of winter-dead grass, which undulated in the rain-driven wind to the horizon. Throughout the morning thick gray clouds fled to the south and around midmorning the sun broke through. Molly could see that spring had streaked the hills with dewy-green resplendence, and she found some solace in the beauty around her.

"Would you go to New Orleans if you could?" Emily asked.

"I can't go anywhere until I know where Emmet is," Molly replied.

"If Emmet was here, do you think he would go?"

"I don't think you could keep him away, Emily. I don't think he's cut out for farming. He misses the life, but even if he wanted to go, you'd never get Innis to agree."

"I can get Innis to do anything I want."

"I don't see how."

"I'll find a way to outsmart him."

"That's not that easy to do, Emily."

"I can do it. I outsmarted him at the Mardi Gras, didn't I?"

"You were seventeen. Things are different now. You weren't married to him then. That's when you met him, isn't it? Didn't you say it was Fat Tuesday? You told me about that but you never told me you outsmarted him."

"Okay, Molly, it was like this. I was wearing that white gown you helped me make. Do you remember?"

"Yes."

"When Innis saw me in that white gown, he came up wearing a robber's disguise and a black mask that he held over his eyes on a stick. He pulled a neckerchief up over his nose and mouth and said he wanted to steal my heart."

"I can see why," Molly added. "You always were a pretty girl, prettier than me, and he's a handsome man. But, I don't see how that outsmarted him."

"You're pretty, too, Molly. You're taller than me and you have those high cheekbones, like a princess."

Molly laughed. "A princess in rags, you mean?"

Emily continued, "I told him I was saving my heart for someone else and I would not dance with him. That's how I outsmarted him. So, he decided he wanted to be first to find the little baby in the king cake. The Padre said the boy who finds it would get special dance privileges. He could choose any girl he wanted to dance with. You should have seen Innis gobble that king cake, Molly. He pulled off that neckerchief, and ate king cake faster than his cheeks could hold it. Everyone was laughing at him and at the others too. There were other boys who wanted to dance with me. Then he ran up with that little porcelain baby and chose me for the dance."

"That's not outsmarting him," Molly pointed out. "You were just being hard to get, and if I remember right, he gave you a real baby a couple years after that. I think he's the one who outsmarted you."

"Baby Amy," Emily agreed.

"Knowing what you know now," Molly asked, "would you do anything different? That is, if you could do things over?"

"Well," Emily mused. "There was that boy wearing the harlequin costume. He was the one standing behind Innis."

"I can hear you," Innis called to them from the other side of the wagon.

Emily smiled and clapped her hands over her mouth.

"I think you're right about you-know-where," Molly whispered, glancing over at Innis, and hoping that he couldn't hear. "I always liked working with you. We're good together. You're a good seamstress and the work is good you-know-where. We were always inside where it was warm and dry. We didn't have to walk in mud up to our ankles all day, like we are now."

"Yes," Emily added. "It was warm and dry, but it wasn't always so good. Did I ever tell you what Madam LaMonte did to me?"

"Yes, you did. You ranted about Madam LaMonte for weeks."

"I wasn't ranting, Molly. I thought I told you what she did?"

"You said she cheated you." Expecting to hear another tedious story from her baby sister, Molly didn't refuse her and decided it would help pass the time. She'd practically raised Emily and loved her. She always listened to everything she had to say, and proceeded to ask, "So, how did she cheat you?"

"You don't remember, do you?"

"No, I guess I don't. It's been too long, Emily?"

"She wanted me to make clothes for her house servants. Everything had to be white with button up collars, and aprons with lacy fronts, very fancy. And, I had to make a suit for the butler. But, when it came time to pay me for the extra clothes, she wouldn't give me anything. She said it was part of our agreement. She cheated me out of two weeks work."

"Now I remember. And yes, you are ranting."

"I'm not ranting, Molly. I was going to tell you how I outsmarted her."

"Like you outsmarted Innis?"

"No, how I outsmarted Madam LaMonte. She'd find fault with everything I did. She'd say, 'You're not going to leave it that way, are you?'" Emily used a squeaky, arrogant voice to imitate Madam LaMonte.

Amused by the change in Emily's voice, Molly chuckled.

"It started with those cursed button holes in her dress," Emily continued. "I made them with cotton thread instead of silk, like she wanted. She never told me she wanted silk thread, just assumed I would know. She said, 'Mister LaMonte is paying you good wages to work for me, and I expect better work than that. Take that thread out and do it over, and do it right this time or I'll have to send you home without your pay.'

"She said that all the time, Molly, about everything I did, no matter how good it was. She'd always find something wrong with it. 'This collar isn't straight! Fix it! These cuffs aren't long enough! Fix it, or I'll send you home without out your pay!'"

Molly held up her hand, and said, "I've heard all this before, Emily, and I'm sorry it happened to you. But, that's just the way rich people are. They're never happy. You can't please them no matter what you do. They always complain, and most of them will cheat you when they can, and apparently she did. You always said you wanted to open a boutique in New Orleans, but you knew that your customers would be rich people. I'm beginning to wonder if you can handle rich people."

"Oh, I can handle them all right. Believe me. I can handle them just fine, like I handled Madam LaMonte."

"You said you outsmarted her."

"I did. I ate breakfast and lunch every day with the house-servants. In the evening they always invited me to join the family at their dinner table. That's when Madam LaMonte would start in on me. One time she said, 'I've seen grain sacks that look better than that dress or those britches you made today. Herman, can't you find something for her to do out in the barn. Why can't you have her work with the slaves and make grain sacks? She'd be good at that.'

"Then her youngsters would laugh at me. They thought it was very funny. I wanted to crawl under the table and hide sometimes. I was so embarrassed. Then Madam LaMonte's teeth went bare one day and she said, 'The only reason you're here, Emily, is because my husband likes you.'

"Then Mister LaMonte stuck up for me. 'That's enough,' he said."

Emily mimicked his deep, manly voice, and this also amused Molly.

"'She's the finest seamstress in a hundred miles and she comes with the highest recommendations. She will stay here until her work is finished, whether you like it or not. I won't hear any more about it, Fredericka.'

"Then he went back to eating his supper and it was a good one too, roasted beef, sweet potatoes, carrots and gravy. Madam LaMonte just sat there, glaring at him. After supper I went back to work, like I always did, and after that I went to bed. They let me stay in the guest room upstairs. Then I would get up every morning and go to work again."

Molly felt a flush of anger rise on her cheeks, as she responded, "You just sat there and took that from her? You let her get away with treating you like that? I would have quit. I would have got up from their supper table and walked out on her then and there and let her sew her own clothing. I will not bend my knee to moneyed aristocracy."

"I didn't bend my knee to her, Molly. I was just doing what I had to do. I was doing my part to earn enough money, so we could all come to Texas and buy land. The part I never told you is how I outsmarted her. I never said anything, because it embarrasses me when I think about it. I did a really mean thing and I probably need to apologize for doing it. See, they had this big giant dog. I don't know what he was exactly, but he stood almost as tall as me, and he had long hair. Some kind of hound I've never heard of."

"A wolf hound?" Molly asked.

"Yes. That's what Mister LaMonte called him. He was proud as punch of that dog, 'a true-blue hunter,' he called him. And, Madam LaMonte called him her 'Little Oscar.' In the afternoon he'd plop down in front of her rocking chair on that hardwood floor in the parlor. She'd kick off her shoes, and open her book. Then she'd prop her feet up on Little Oscar, and rock her feet back and forth on him until Miss Sarah called her for supper. He loved it, and he'd snore, mercy sakes, he'd snore until the dust shook off the candelabras."

Molly held her hand up again. "Emily! You're not saying you did something to their dog, are you?"

"Well, yes. I guess I am. I had to."

OSCAR

"I CAN'T BELIEVE what I'm hearing," Molly told Emily. "You did something to their dog? I can't believe you'd hurt their dog."

"I didn't hurt him," Emily explained. "He was my buddy. Whenever Madam LaMonte was out doing things, he wanted to snuggle up to me under the sewing table. It was a nice big table, too. I could spread a dress out on it. It made my work a lot easier. I wish I had a table like that."

"You didn't hurt him then?"

"No! Of course not. I'm not the monster you think I am."

"I don't think you're a monster, Emily. You know that."

"So anyway, Sarah would bring me breakfast, that is, after the family was finished. We usually had fresh henhouse eggs and grits, and we always had bacon and tea. Those servants could smoke up the best side of bacon I ever had, and they wouldn't give me the recipe either. They said it was the only secret they had. Sometimes they gave me hot cakes.

"One time Sarah asked me, 'Missus Carrigan, would y'all like one of Master LaMonte's packled aggs?'

"Sure, I says. So, she opened the lid on this big old crock in the kitchen, and fished out one of those pickled eggs. It was the worst thing I ever saw, Molly. Have you ever seen a pickled egg?"

"No," Molly admitted, "but it doesn't sound that bad."

"Well, it was. They turn all green and purple in that crock, and they smell like something you'd find in the barnyard. I thanked Sarah for it, and just left it sitting on my plate. Did I tell you that they used china for their everyday dishes? I've never seen such a thing. Do you know how much china costs? Probably five or six dollars per setting, that's more than I make in a month. And, have mercy on the poor girl that broke something.

"One time I heard something break out in the kitchen, and I heard the girls scramble around to clean it up before Madam LaMonte found it, but it was too late. She heard it break and came running. She screeched at them something awful, Molly, and she wanted to whip the girl that broke it, but no one fessed up. And I don't blame them either. I wouldn't have fessed up either. They stood their ground. Madam LaMonte, she punished them all for it. She made them wash and polish every dish and every piece of silver in the house, and watched over them while they did it, and she would have whipped anyone who dropped anything. It took them all day. Then they had to cook supper, clean up, and go to bed with nothing to eat. I was invited to join the family that night for supper, but I couldn't eat anything. I lost my appetite."

"So, what about the pickled egg?" Molly asked. "Did you eat it?"

"Heavens no. I gave it to Oscar after Sarah went back in the kitchen. He loved it, too. He rolled over on his back and dangled his feet up in the air after I gave it to him. You'd think he was eating a beef loin or something. First thing every morning he'd crawl under the sewing table and wait for it, and I'd give it to him, too. After lunch, he'd go to the parlor and wait for Madam LaMonte. She'd go in there, kick off her shoes and start rocking.

"Then pretty soon I'd hear Madam LaMonte say, 'Whew, Oscar what's the matter with you?' Then she'd holler, 'Sarah! Sarah! Would you take Oscar outdoors so he can take care of his business? He has to go.'"

Molly laughed, choked, and grabbed her sides. "Oh, Emily. You're terrible."

"Well Molly, I think Sarah figured out what I was doing, because she'd bring me that pickled egg every morning without asking if I wanted it. And, she'd always have that smile on her face, not the courteous kind of smile she gave everyone else, but a smile that said, 'I know what you're going to do with that egg.'

"After she'd take Oscar outdoors, he'd go right back in the parlor with Madam LaMonte. I could hear her put her feet up on him and start rocking again. Before long she'd say, 'Whew, Oscar, did you do that again?' Then she'd holler at Sarah, 'Did you take him outdoors, Sarah? I think he still has to go.'"

Molly had to stop walking for a moment. From her hands her hem slipped into the mud. Bending over, she clasped her arms around her stomach, making nary a noise except for a snorting sound, which she couldn't help. "Emily, please," she pleaded. "Don't tell me anymore."

"You all right over there?" Innis asked from the other side of the wagon. "This ain't no time for laughing and carrying on. Will y'all get moving? We have to keep moving."

Picking her hem out of the mud, Molly shook it and plodded forward. Resuming her pace, she realized that the sun had dried her clothes, and now she was too warm. Pulling the stiff, dry quilt from her shoulders, she tossed it in the wagon. Then she shook heavy clods of mud from the ruffles on her pantalets. Shaking them off didn't help much, since the mud continued to collect as she walked.

Emily shook clods from her pantalets, grabbed up the hem of her dress, and said, "We thought farm chores were hard, didn't we, Molly? Bet you never dreamed we'd wind up doing this."

Palming tears from her eyes, Molly thought about Oscar the dog, tried to speak, but could only laugh when she opened her mouth.

"That's how I outsmarted Madam LaMonte," Emily explained, with pride in her voice. "I gave that pickled egg to Oscar every morning until I finished up with the LaMonte family. And now, when I think about it, I don't care if she never paid me for the servants' clothes. It was worth it to outsmart her."

Understanding that Emily hadn't actually outsmarted Madam LaMonte, Molly knew the pickle egg had been vengeful and Emily had used it as a way to repay Madam LaMonte for her perceived mistreatment. Nevertheless, she agreed with her little sister's puerile reasoning, and said, "Yes, Emily, you outsmarted her, and I'm proud of you."

Lowering her gaze to her shoes, Molly watched mud splash over the tops and onto her legs and pantalets. Her feet squished inside. The mud never seemed to end and deepened where rivulets washed over the road.

Glancing over at Emily, she said, "You were upset about losing our homes last night. I know I'm upset. But, you don't seem so upset today."

"I was last night, Molly, but not anymore. When we first came here I was excited about owning our farm, but now I'm just looking forward to whatever comes next, waiting to see what's ahead. I believe this is all happening for a reason. I know that whatever is coming will be better. I can't see the answer right now, but I will in time." Emily swung her hem back and forth, saying, "I will in time."

"I wish I could see things the way you do," Molly sighed. "The only thing I see ahead is someone waiting to knock me down every time I pick myself up. Sometimes I think I'd be better off if I just stayed down. There'd be a lot less disappointment that way."

"Sure there would," Emily quipped, with a hint of sarcasm in her voice. "Maybe, we should have stayed in Gonzales!"

Glancing over at her, Molly scowled.

"I'm sorry you feel that way, Molly. You really don't believe there's a reason for this, do you?"

"No, I don't!" Molly admitted.

Cresting the first rise, they descended into a shallow vale where rivulets converged into a grassy flow, which covered the road. It appeared stable until a horse stepped into it. Gumbo, the men-folk called it, Texas gumbo. Some of the soldiers had waded in waist deep, and stood by to assist the town folks, as they crossed. Innis tightened the reins and led the horses in. They slid in deep, spooked and bolted, sending up a spray of gumbo, and pulling Innis off his feet by the reins. Sprawling headfirst, he flayed his arms in mud deeper than his arms were long. Standing and dripping gumbo from his face, hair, and clothing, he scooped mud from his eyes. Then he retrieved his hat, shook it off, and set it on his head. Looking back at Emily, he must have noticed something about the way she looked at him because he hollered, "Are you laughing at me, woman?"

Emily shook her head, Molly bit her lip, and neither of them laughed at his misfortune.

Xavier had fallen over in the wagon with the youngsters when it lurched, which set the youngsters to screaming for their mothers. Taking

Amy into her arms, Emily's eyes bulged and appeared ready to pop, but she did not laugh at Innis.

Refugees, old and small, waded into the mud while soldiers helped Innis push the wagon across. Even the women pulled at the spokes to get the wheels turning. The older youngsters and their mothers waded in, carrying the littlest ones.

Xavier led his mule in, its load swayed back and forth. He stumbled, and a soldier threw his arm around him to keep him from falling, and then walked with him to the other side.

The gumbo pulled at Molly's shoes when she lifted her feet, but the length of the lacing, up past her ankles, kept them on. A youngster stumbled with his little brother. She watched helplessly as they both scrambled out of the gumbo bawling, covered with slop, and looking very much as Innis had looked. Their shoes were gone, stuck somewhere in the goo.

Xavier's daughter-in-law stumbled, but managed to keep herself from falling with her toddler, in spite of losing her shoes. A soldier tried to retrieve the shoes with a shovel, but was not able to lift the shovel against the suction of the mud. The effort was useless. All together, the older youngsters and two of the mothers in the Carrigan group lost their shoes and had to continue their journey barefoot from then on.

Xavier's daughter-in-law pumped her knees through the gumbo, carrying her toddler alongside Molly and whimpering, "You've led us astray in the Slough of Despond."

"Maudie!" Molly snapped at her. "I haven't led you anywhere. You might think you're in the Slough of Despond, but you're not! The Slough of Despond is a place where folks give up. I haven't given up, and you shouldn't either!"

When the little ones and Xavier were again in the wagon, Innis cracked the reins. Ascending and descending the next rise, they came abruptly to another flow of gumbo over the road. The refugees carried the little ones and Innis led the horses by their bridles. Innis had many opportunities to improve his mud hole crossing skills, and became proficient at it by the time he reached the Lavaca River later that evening.

The Lavaca was swollen with rain and impassable. Fortunately, the road turned and followed the top of the banks to a crossing place where the water was shallow and fast, and the bottom was solid. Across the river, General Houston had his soldiers direct the town folks into Williamson Daniels' meadow for the night.

In the morning the sun glared horizontally through the trees, as Innis drove the wagon into line. Emily sat between him and Molly, with Amy on her lap. Powerful gusts brought heavy clouds and thick sheets of spring rain throughout the day. Deepening mud forced Molly and the refugees out of the wagon again, and the next two days they struggled through the mud, most of them barefoot. Sleeping where they could, they were unable to build a fire. Nothing was dry enough to burn. So, they ate cold salt-pork, chewed on waterlogged corn, and remained soaked to the skin, cold, and shivering.

Some of the littlest youngsters acquired the sniffles and a cough, and in the following days others were given to long bouts of coughing. Molly noticed the tell tale whistle, which accompanied their coughs, and warned Emily, "Keep Amy with you. Keep her away from the other youngsters. We'll take turns with her, okay." She'd heard whooping cough before, and with the wet and cold conditions they had to endure, she knew the youngster's survival could become uncertain.

Emily took Amy from the wagon and carried her. In turn Molly also carried her through the mud.

The stitches began to rot out of Molly's wet shoes. Tearing away from the front uppers, the soles opened when she lifted her feet, allowing her shoes to fill with gumbo and manure from the road. When she set her feet down, they squished out. But, she felt fortunate. Maudie was bare foot and bleeding. Xavier had cut pieces from his bedroll to bind her feet, but she had to continually retie the bindings.

Some of the youngsters used whatever they could find to bind their bleeding feet, sometimes using the clothes they were wearing. Molly wrapped and tied up the fronts of her shoes with strips she'd cut from an empty grain sack. The remainder of the sack she cut into strips and distributed to those who had need.

At the Navidad River, the LaBahia Road split off north from the Atascosito Road. There Molly and the Carrigan refugees spent another night without fire in the relentless, cold rain. To the sideboards of the wagon the refugees tied their quilts and blankets and stretched them to the ground, making a shelter. Filling the water barrel in the muddy Navidad, they replenished their water supply for the coming day, while Molly opened the salt-pork barrel.

She discovered that the youngsters had been helping themselves to the salt-pork throughout the last couple days and most of it was gone. Without complaining, she divided what was left, about a handful each, among the refugees. They were thankful to have it. She noticed that the womenfolk and youngsters were looking gaunt, and many were spending more time than usual dashing into the bushes. When they were all under the dripping shelter, they huddled together for warmth until morning.

Waking up semi-dry, Molly wasn't as cold as when her journey began, but she was very hungry. Saturated with mud, her dress was looser than when she started. She wondered if it had stretched and felt around her waist, noticing how thin she'd become in less than a week.

Underway without breakfast, the youngsters traveling with them began to complain about their lack of food. Oblivious to hunger, the littlest ones coughed and whistled as their mothers tried to comfort them.

Walking the wagon onto the road, Innis didn't have to wait in line for an army escort this morning, as he had the previous days. Walking alongside Emily and with Amy in her arms, Molly noticed that folks were already passing them, many new folks, whom she didn't recognize from other settlements. Scurrying past, some of them drove wagons, others drove two-wheeled carts, and some led packhorses. Many carried their belongings tied to their backs.

Ahead, Molly noticed a woman with a small boy and an older man driving a wagon. Then she recognized the tiny strawberry mole. "Elli-Lou Susser," Molly yelled. Uncle Elmer was turning north, up the LaBahia Road. "Hold up a minute, Innis," Molly insisted. Wading through the mud over to Elli-Lou's wagon, she said, "I lost track of you. I'm sorry we got separated back in Gonzales. We never had a chance to talk after that first night."

"It's okay, Molly. Things are a lot worse than I thought they would be. Maybe someday, when the war is over, we can have some time together again."

"I miss those times, Elli-Lou."

"So do I, Molly."

"Where are you going?"

"Uncle Elmer wants to go up to Cole's Settlement, says he knows folks up there. Then we'll probably go to my Cousin Ike's farm in Louisiana."

"Good luck, Elli-Lou. I hope Franklin finds you up there."

"I'll pray that Emmet finds you too, Molly."

Molly caught up with Emily again.

Innis cracked the reins and walked beside the wagon. Glancing over at Emily and Molly, he recalled, "I passed a freight-hauler one time, and he told me he knew Texas from border to border, and from the top to the bottom of every mud hole." Innis smiled. "He was chest deep in mud at the time, and cracking whip on a team of horses."

"There's going to be more mud, isn't there?" Emily cringed and squished her foot down into the mud on the road in front of her.

"Most likely," he replied. "They don't call the Atascosito 'the Old Boggy' for nothing, and it's been raining heavy."

About a hundred paces up the road a wagon had pulled off in the weeds. Molly could see women standing in the wagon, and facing each other. Between them they held up a blanket, as if to shelter someone from the rain. Concerned that someone had been injured or had fallen ill, Molly prepared to offer what assistance she could.

A lone man waded toward her, walking against the flow of fleeing refugees. Molly paused as he drew near and asked, "Aren't y'all going the wrong way?"

Hesitating, he explained, "I'm going back home. Got to get my kin away from there. Got to get them where it's safe."

"Are you a soldier?" Molly asked.

"Yes, ma'am."

"You're the only soldier I've seen this morning. Yesterday there were hundreds of soldiers on the road. Where are they all now? Where did they all go?"

ROOT HOG OR DIE

THE SOLDIER COUGHED into his hand, turned and spit on the ground. Molly noticed purple coloration below his puffy eyes and sensed that he was not well. Reaching out to him, she asked, "Are you all right? Do you need help?"

"Obliged, ma'am, but I'll be okay. Just need to get home."

"Why is General Houston letting you go?" she questioned.

"He didn't, ma'am. I left on my own, like everyone else. I have to take care of my family. I didn't think things would go like this, ma'am. I figured we could stop Santa Anna back at the Rio Grande before he crossed over into Texas, or I figured we could stop him at the Alamo. Now he's stomping through Texas on one side, whilst Houston is burning us out on the other side."

"Yes, I know," Molly informed him. "I'm from Gonzales."

"I'm afeard, ma'am, there won't be nothing left but ashes when this fight is over. Whether we win or lose, we're all going to lose everything."

"You're saying that all the soldiers deserted?" Molly asked.

"Houston took what's left of the troops up to Beason's Crossing for 'organizing and training,' he says. I think there's about three hundred of us that decided to skedaddle home, so now he don't have many reinforcements left. Scouts are saying that Santa Anna has split his army into three forces. They said he sent General Urrea with one force down to Victoria, and he sent General Gaona up the Camino Real to Nacogdoches with another one. Santa Anna himself is a coming right up the middle after

General Houston and what's left of his troops. That covers just about everything in Texas, ma'am, so things ain't looking too good. Best thing you can do is keep moving fast as you can, and get across the Sabine into Louisiana, if you want to save your family and your own hide."

Innis had pulled the wagon over into the weeds and stopped when he reached Molly and the soldier. He had been listening to the soldier, and mumbled, "That's about what I figured. We should stay with Houston. We're just going to draw trouble out here in the open like this."

The soldier nodded his agreement. "Problem is I don't think you folks can move fast enough to catch him, and y'all need to put up a guard too. This here country is overrun with Santa Anna's scouts and the Comancheros he's hiring. They know the land, and they figure we're easy pickings. The Comancheros are committing depredations everywhere they go. I figure they're watching us right now, and waiting for a chance to take what little we got left. I also heard that the Comanches might have joined up with them to drive us out. They want our land, and the Comancheros have been trading them rifles, too. You folks need to stay together and protect each other until y'all get across the Sabine."

"Obliged." Innis shook the soldier's hand.

The soldier resumed his journey.

As Innis drove the wagon out of the weeds onto the Atascosito, Molly recognized the wagon ahead in which womenfolk had sheltered someone. It was the Schauble's wagon. The person under the shelter was Missis Schauble, and she was tending Maria Benson who was, at this very moment, giving birth. Molly approached the rear of the wagon and asked Misses Schauble, "Do you need help? Can I do anything?"

Innis pulled his wagon into the weeds again.

Missis Schauble gave Molly a quick, sideways glance, and said, "Hey, Molly McCracken." Slapping a tiny newborn infant ever so gently, she smiled as the baby took its first breath and cried. "Y'all can come in here and help Maria whilst I wrap this little one in a blanket." Missis Schauble held the infant up for Molly to see, and declared, "It's a girl." Then she proceeded to clean the infant with a rag, and explain, "I had to get rid of a few things to make room for a bed back here. Maria has to stay off her feet. So, watch where you're walking out there in the weeds. Don't trip over anything."

Furniture, clothing and personal items were strewn around the wagon, where Missis Schauble had thrown them out. Molly stepped over the items and climbed in to help. When the newborn was in Maria's arms, the other women climbed out and allowed Maria's boys to hold a shelter of blankets over her. Then Molly climbed out.

Mister Titus Schauble looked back at Molly, and the elderly man's voice trembled as he said, "Looks like y'all got things under control back here." His furrowed brow, flaring nostrils, and the gray moustache, which seemed to grow out from them, made his appearance unmistakable.

A pillar in Gonzales, Molly always thought of him as temperate, worthy of respect and self-controlled. She would have liked him as her grandfather. She replied, "You're an admirable man, Mister Schauble. You seem to be taking all this very well."

He chuckled. "I'm doing alright, considering everything that's happened."

"You lost your mercantile."

"Yes." He chuckled again, his voice faltering a little. "Oh yes, but there's more important things than that old mercantile, isn't there, Molly? I'm just glad we can help Maria here, and her youngins, and I'm glad we're all safe."

Missis Schauble stepped up next to him, and he cracked his reins. Smiling back at Molly, he hollered, "Good day, Missis McCracken. Obliged for your help."

Behind the Schaubles, Innis drove his wagon again onto the road. Emily and the Carrigan refugees trudged through the mud beside him. Glancing around at the things the Schauble's had left behind, Molly noticed they were good things, valuable things, and things she'd like to have at home, but neither had she room for them in the Carrigan farm wagon, not with all the sick youngsters and infirm adults aboard. Her eyes caught on a small box with dovetail corners. Nothing was inside, but the container was sturdy, probably used for shipping something small, but important. She could use it to organize a few small things in the sea-chest. So she tucked it under her arm and caught up with Emily.

The road had clogged with fleeing refugees creating long lines at mud holes and river crossings. Nothing could the Carrigans and their refugees do but wait. They couldn't go forward or backward, and they were tired, nodding off and jolting awake as they waited for the wagons ahead to move. Without the assistance of the soldiers, the womenfolk and their youngsters had to push their wagons through by themselves, adding an additional three days to the Carrigans journey to San Felipe. Innis decided to walk ahead and assist at the next mud hole. Xavier agreed to drive the wagon for him, and those who were able joined Innis, helping push refugees through until the Carrigan wagon had been pushed across.

The rain began to let up, and the sun came out, but the road remained muddy. Searching for high ground, Innis found a suitable place to camp and for the first time in many nights he and his refugees were able to build a fire and cook some of their rain soaked corn.

"I'm going to keep watch tonight," Innis said, as he helped himself to a plate of mush. "Tomorrow I'll catch a nap while were waiting at the mud holes. When we get to San Felipe, we'll be safe."

The next morning Molly was first to rise. She could hear the whistling coughs of youngsters cuddled with their mothers under their blankets around a dwindling campfire. It had been their first dry night in more than a week.

Upon the wagon's seat-board she noticed Innis perched with his rifle across his lap. Climbing up, she greeted him, "Morning."

"You hear that?" he asked.

"Hear what?"

"Turn your ear that-a-way." Up the road he pointed.

She turned, listened, and asked, "Is that cannon?"

"Yes, and I hear rifles too, Molly, lots of them, hundreds of them, all going off at the same time. The wind is carrying the sound of a fight, a big one. I hope it's farther away than I think."

Panic knotted Molly's stomach. "What does this mean?" she asked him. "They're going to overtake us, aren't they? What are we going to do?"

To the ground Innis jumped and yelled, "Come on, folks! We have to get moving! Come on!"

Slowly the refugees rose, some of them rubbing their eyes. Others dashed into the bushes, while many remained asleep on the ground.

"Come on! Let's go!" Innis hollered at them again.

Molly shook Emily's shoulder, rousing her, and watched, as Xavier's daughter-in-law, Maudie, came back from the bushes with her toddler in her arms. The little boy had tucked his hands under his head upon her shoulder and Molly's heart stopped when she realized that his body had no breath in it. "Maudie?" she gasped. "Is he okay?"

"Yes, he's fine." The young mother patted the toddler's back.

"He's not breathing, Maudie, and he's turning blue."

"He's fine," she insisted. "It's just the whooping cough. I think he's getting better. He stopped coughing."

Molly reached out to halt her, and turn her around. Her eyes were blank, and tears streamed down her cheeks. "Let me have him!" Molly pulled the youngster away from her. Leaning him over her arm, she rapped him sharply on his back to clear and restore his breathing. Maudie slipped down onto her knees, buried her face in her hands, and sobbed. Molly held an ear to the toddler's face and listened for his breath, then leaned him over her arm and rapped him on his back again, several times.

Stumbling toward her, Xavier leaned on his walking stick, and asked, "What is this?" His hand trembled as he reached out to his grandson. "What is this?" he asked again.

"I'm so sorry," Molly handed the lifeless toddler to him. "There wasn't anything I could do."

Letting loose of his walking stick, it fell to the ground. Into his arms he took the toddler, and then plopped down next to Maudie, rocking his grandson on his lap. "This is no good place for him. No good place," he said.

On Maudie's shoulder Molly laid her hand to comfort her. Emily joined them with Amy, but stood back. Others gathered around, as Innis rushed over. Pulling his hat from his head, he said, "I was afraid something like this would happen. I wish there was a way to keep things like this from happening to us." Kneeling down, he looked into Xavier's face, and explained the situation, "We're in trouble here, my friend. I'm sorry this happened to you, and Maudie, and your grandson. But, y'all have to understand that Santa Anna is coming right up this road behind us. About all I can do is help you bury him. Would you like me to do that?"

"Gracias, Señor Carrigan. This is very kind of you."

Standing, Innis added, "We don't have much time."

Refugees rushed past the camp in wagons, carts, and pack animals, as the Carrigan refugees assisted with the burial, and offered prayers around the toddler's grave. As Innis filled in the little grave, Emily stood by clutching Amy to her chest and said, "It looks like all we can do now is pray."

Molly clenched her teeth until her jaw ached, and then replied, "Y'all go ahead and pray, Emily. And, while you're praying, why don't you ask the Almighty why he isn't doing anything about this? We're good folks and we don't deserve this. That little boy didn't do anything wrong. Maudie and Xavier over there, look at them, they're good folks, too. They don't deserve this either."

Emily did not respond, only watched and listened to Molly's rant, and in her eyes Molly could see disappointment.

As the road began to dry, Molly, Emily and Amy were able to ride again on the seat-board with Innis. The sick and infirm rode in back. Those who were able had to run at times to keep up with them.

Innis drove the wagon hard until he encountered a crowd of womenfolk blocking the road. It was about midmorning. Steering the wagon into the brush, he bypassed them. Molly noticed that the womenfolk were standing around an open grave at the side of the road and said, "Innis, we have to stop and help them."

"Go ahead and help them," he replied, "but I ain't stopping until I get to San Felipe."

Molly couldn't believe his refusal to help.

Driving the horses out of the brush and onto the road, he jostled the wagon, which brought cries and fits of coughing from the youngsters in back.

Emily screamed at him, "Innis Carrigan, you stop this wagon right now and help these poor womenfolk."

Pulling back the reins, the horses whinnied, as he stopped the wagon by the women at the gravesite, and grumbled, "If I stop, there'll be more graves along this road than just this one."

"What do you mean?" one of the mourners asked him.

"I mean Santa Anna's right behind us. I heard cannon and rifle this morning."

The women gasped.

He added, "Y'all better let the dead bury the dead, and get yourselves moving."

Emily cocked her elbow, stomped her foot on the floorboards, and yelled, "You help them, Innis, or you'll be the one that's dead."

"Don't be talking to me like that, woman," he huffed. Then from behind the seat-board he grabbed his shovel and leapt to the ground, filling the grave in haste.

A weary looking woman leaned on her shovel, sweat dripping from her brow, as she said, "Bless you, sir."

"This ain't no time for blessing, ma'am. You folks need to finish up your praying and get along while you still can."

When he was again under way, Molly looked back and saw that the womenfolk were scrambling into their wagon. Throughout the afternoon and into the evening, Innis stopped only long enough to water and graze the horses.

"Aren't you going to make camp?" Emily asked him.

"Can't," he huffed. "This might be our only chance to outrun Santa Anna. We have to keep going. It can't be much farther to San Felipe."

Well past sunset he continued to drive, the way illuminated by twilight until Molly could see the road no more. The moon and stars were not sufficient to continue, but she could see campfires flickering ahead on the plain. Unable to travel further in the dark, Innis turned his frothy horses off the road, as his refugees limped up the road behind him.

Molly and Emily climbed down into the brush. Emily slapped her cheek, then her neck, and said, "Now the mosquitoes are after us."

"Is Amy covered up?" Molly asked.

"Yes, she's asleep under the seat-board. I wrapped her in a quilt. Can you help me clear a place for a fire?"

Hounds ululated from the nearby camps and a gunshot startled Molly. The popping gunshot was followed by another loud, echoing pop. Emily screamed, "Santa Anna is attacking us. What do we do?"

In the direction of the shots Molly spun and looked into the darkness. She could see shadowy figures among a stand of trees by a campfire. One of them was hunched over a body. "I think I know who that is," she said.

Grabbing up his rifle, Innis bounded past her, running straight for the campfire where the shadows lurked. Into the darkness he faded. Molly heard him crashing through the brush.

"Los caballos! Prisa!" someone shouted.

The crashing stopped. Molly assumed that Innis had paused, unseen, and she feared that he was in grave danger. A flash illuminated the stand of barren trees, and the crack of a rifle startled her. A man screamed, expelling a frightening sound that raised goose hairs on Molly's forearms.

"Te me disparó, hijo de cerdo!" the man yelled.

Horses crashed through the brush straight at her and Emily. When Innis leapt from the brush, she breathed a sigh of relief, for it was Innis crashing toward her, and not horses.

"I need to reload," he announced. Leaping into the wagon, he fumbled through the sea-chest in the dark, taking out his powder horn and ball.

Molly didn't understand how he could see what he was doing.

"I got one of them," he said.

"Sí, you got one of them, Señor Carrigan," Xavier agreed, as he dropped an armload of firewood next to the wagon, "I hear him. I think he say, 'You shot me, you son of a pig." Xavier smoothed his mustache with his forefinger and thumb, and added, "I think you got him pretty good."

"Who were they?" Molly asked.

"Don't know for sure," Innis replied, "robbers or looters, I think." His hands and his voice shook. Dropping his powder horn, he mumbled, "Darn it," and felt around on the floorboards of the wagon until finding it again.

Molly tugged on Emily's sleeve, and said, "I have to see what's wrong in that camp over there. Will you come with me, please?"

"That ain't a good idea," Innis cautioned her. "There might be more of them out there. Get down in the wagon until we know what's happening out there. After I reload, I'll go back out. You should stay here until I come back."

"That's Missis Schauble over there," Molly insisted. "I recognize her. I'm going over there. I can tell that something is terribly wrong. We owe her, Innis. How many times has she given us medicine when we were sick, or given us credit when we didn't have any money? She's good folk, and other folks are always taking advantage of good folk, like her, and never giving back. Well, I'm giving back, Innis. I'm going over there."

"She's right," Emily agreed. "I'm going with her."

Molly lifted the hem of her mud caked dress and stomped into the darkness. Close behind, Emily joined her. Innis followed a few paces back, as he pushed a rifle ball into place with a ramrod. Through the brush they stumbled in the dark, sidestepping a patch of Prickly Pear, from which Molly had to untangle her pantalets.

When they reached the light of the Schauble campfire, they found Titus Schauble lying on his back in a grassy space where he'd made camp. His thin nose pointed toward the sky, and his nostrils pointed toward the fire. Beside him Missis Schauble knelt over him and wept. Maria Benson, with her infant and her five boys, watched nearby.

"What happened?" Molly asked.

"He was sitting right here by the fire," Missis Schauble howled. "I seen someone climbing out of the wagon. Then I heard a shot, and Titus just shut his eyes and fell back. Whatever that scoundrel wanted, I would of give it to him if he'd asked for it. He didn't have to shoot. I seen others running off too, so I pulled out my old dueling pistol and shot back at them." She patted the butt of a pistol behind a sash around her waist. "Now my poor Titus is lying here dead. This ain't right, Molly. It just ain't right." Shaking her head, she laid her hands on him, and beneath her billowing sleeves Molly could see her frail shoulders heaving.

When the Carrigan refugees caught up, they entered the Schauble camp with other folks who stumbled in. All converged at about the same time, and gathered around Mister Schauble. Kneeling over him, Molly grasped his shoulders, pressed her ear against his chest, and declared, "He's gone."

"I know," Missis Schauble's voice quavered. "What am I going to do?" Standing when Molly stood, she was then embraced by the womenfolk at the campsite as old men dabbed tears from their eyes.

Henry Hort stepped up, halting and bent, with his rifle in hand, saying, "Evening, folks. I'm camped over yonder. Heard the shooting. Did y'all see who it was, Missis Schauble?"

"It was dark, Henry, but I seen a stout man with bushy hair and a pointed beard."

"All right then, I'll go have a look around."

"I'll go with you." Innis offered.

Molly asked Missis Schauble, "Did you know that Santa Anna is right behind us?"

"I've been hearing such."

"Do you have any kin you can go to from here, anyone you can stay with?"

"I ain't had no kin since the Green Flag Rebellion back in eighteen-twelve." From the pocket of her soiled dress she pulled a hanky and dried her tears, tucked her thin, gray hair under her lacy bonnet, and continued, "Titus is the only one of our clan that came back from the Battle of Medina. Back then we had to flee north from General Arrendondo. Now it looks like everything is repeating itself all over again with that murderous Santa Anna on our tail. Here we go, root hog or die, just like before, like we've all come down with the runaway fever."

"Yes." Molly agreed. "I've heard about those things. They happened before I came to Texas. You never told me much about what happened."

"I lost four strong boys, an uncle, and a brother at Medina. It broke my heart for a long time. I should of got used to folks killing each other here abouts, but I never got used to it, Molly. Things settled down after awhile. Then we came back to start over. That's when we built the mercantile, me and Titus. We was too old to have more youngins. We would of liked more youngins, but we thought of other folks' youngins, like they was our grand-youngins. That was good enough. I ain't got no other kin." Lowering her head, she began to weep again.

Embracing her, Molly said, "I think of you like my own grandma, Missis Schauble. I won't leave you like this, none of us will. Me and the other folks here will take care of Mister Schauble, okay."

The town folks donated a quilt to use as Mister Schauble's cerement, and they dug for him a suitable grave. Making the night short, and the morning hours wee, they laid Mister Titus Schauble to rest. After offering prayers, they filled his grave.

"Tomorrow," Molly suggested to Missis Schauble, "you can ride with us, if you like. We'll get you to San Felipe where we'll all be safe. You'll see."

"Obliged, Molly, but I'll be all right. I'll drive my own wagon with my own horses. It's all I got left. I've got Maria here with me, and if I need help, her boys will help me."

Innis returned from the brush with Henry and informed them, "We can't see nothing out there. Must be they can see in the dark, because they sure snuck off on us."

He took Emily back to camp and Molly followed reluctantly, not wanting to leave Missis Schauble in her time of grief. At camp the Carrigan refugees had already built a fire and hung a pot of corn over it. Innis added wood to drive the mosquitoes away, while the womenfolk cared for their sick youngsters.

"We might as well get some rest while we can," Innis suggested, "and leave at first light."

Emily glanced over at the wagon, and said, "I should check on Amy." Climbing up, she looked under the seat-board and screamed, "Innis! Come over here! Please! Come quickly!"

SAN FELIPE

RUNNING TO EMILY'S side, Innis asked, "What's wrong?"

"She's gone!" Emily screamed. "I can't find Amy! She's gone!"

Clasping her shoulders, he suggested, "She's probably just wandered off. Let's check around first."

Looking in the wagon and under it, Emily then searched the brush around the camp. Molly went out toward the Schauble's, as Innis went even farther out into the brush. He called to Molly in the darkness, asking, "Where are you going?"

"I'm thinking that Amy woke up while we were over there helping Missis Schauble. We didn't have a fire, so she was probably scared in the dark, and the closest fire she could see was the Schauble's fire. So, I'm going over there to look for her. She might have gone that way."

Zigzagging through the brush, she could see that a few town folks remained yet with Missis Schauble. Stumbling over a soft object, she yelled out, "Innis, I think I found her!" Reaching down, Molly groped around in the dark brush until she felt something large, about Amy's size, covered with cloth. Innis crashed through as she lifted the bundle into the light of the stars. Close behind him, Emily ran to see what Molly had found and collapsed when she saw what it was.

Innis knelt to assist, and lifted Emily into his arms, saying, "Emily? It's all right, Emily. It's only a blanket."

Her eyes fluttered, and then opened.

"See," Innis explained. "It's only a blanket."

"It's her quilt," Emily whispered. "I recognize it. I made it for her, and I wrapped her up in it this evening."

"But, she's not here," he argued. "That means she's out there somewhere."

"No she isn't." Lowering her head, Emily added. "If she wandered off, we would have found the quilt in the wagon where she was sleeping. Don't you understand, Innis? Her quilt is out here, because someone dropped it out here." Looking up into the heavens, she cried, "What's happening? Everything was going along just fine. Why is everything going so wrong today?" Lifting her hand to her cheek, she closed her eyes and fainted in his arms. Scooping her up, he stood with her, and carried her into camp.

By the fire Maudie sat with Xavier, mourning the loss of her own toddler, as Molly spread a blanket for Emily. Innis lay Emily upon it, and Molly sat with her, wiping perspiration from her brow with a corner of the blanket.

Through the brush town folks came crashing, and they were armed for trouble. The womenfolk had axes and pitchforks. The oldest Benson boy had his squirrel rifle, and Henry held yet his rifle in hand. "What happened?" Henry asked. "We heard screaming over here. Did the looters come back again?"

"Someone run off with our daughter," Innis replied, "probably the same ones that looted the Schauble's wagon and shot Mister Schauble."

"I'm missing two sacks of grain," one of the women informed them.

"My trunk is gone," another added.

"Why would they take Amy?" Molly wailed. Over her eyes she dragged her sleeve, and then pulled Emily into her arms.

"Comancheros," Henry suggested. "I heard they been raiding and looting settlers along these parts. They're known to trade firearms with the Comanches for pelts and hides, beads and such, and sometimes women, and sometimes youngsters. Then they sell their stuff to freebooters down on the coast. They even trade slaves when they can get them. They ain't nothing but pirates on horses."

"They come up from Mexico, don't they?" Molly questioned him. "I thought slavery was illegal in Mexico. Isn't it illegal?"

Henry rested the butt of his rifle on the ground, and answered, "Y'all take a good look at them big plantations over by San Felipe when we get over that way tomorrow, and explain to me what all them slaves are doing there if slavery is illegal."

"What should we do?" Molly asked.

"All right then." Henry lifted his chin and the snow-white beard covering it and glanced around. "We'll spread out and search the brush for Amy first, just in case she wandered off. Then we'll meet back here, and decide what to do next."

Everyone agreed. Then Henry, some of the womenfolk, and the older youngsters spread out, and began searching for Amy, yelling her name in the darkness. Molly noticed that most went without shoes, and the sight broke her heart, as they limped away with their feet wrapped in bloody, mud-caked rags.

Innis paused before joining the search, lifted his hat, and wiped his brow with his fingers. A long breath escaped from him, as he dropped his gaze to the firewood piled beside the campfire. Angrily, he kicked the woodpile. Then lifting his gaze to the sky, he set his hands on his hips, and watched the stars.

"Innis?" Emily asked, as she stirred in Molly's arms. "Did you find her, Innis? Bring her to me. Please. Bring Amy to me. I want to hold her."

Slapping his hat onto his head, Innis turned to watch deep sobs rising from within Emily. Then he sprang to the wagon. Climbing up, he rummaged through the sea-chest. Into a partly emptied sack of parched-corn he stuffed his powder horn, rifle ball, and a blanket.

"What are you doing?" Molly asked.

"I'm going after them."

"You'll be killed."

"Then I'll die fighting." He jumped from the wagon, snatched up his rifle, and slung the grain-sack over his shoulder.

"Innis please wait," Molly begged him. Jumping up in front of him, she placed her finger tips against his chest and said, "You don't know how many of them there are. There might be others. There's always lots of others with men like that. They run together, and you're not prepared for that. And, it's too dark. You can't track them in the dark, can you?"

"Not likely," he agreed.

"Then you'll wander around all night and lose them, right?"

Hanging his head, Innis let the grain sack slide from his shoulder, and admitted, "I don't know what to do."

Emily rolled onto her side and sobbed.

"We need you here," Molly continued. "You're the only able-bodied man here … And, look at Emily. She's collapsed. You can't leave her grieving like this tonight. Will you please forget about going after the Comancheros right now and help Emily? Wait until the other folks come back. You can decide what to do after that, okay."

"You're right, Molly! You're right!" he huffed. "Why don't you stay here with her while I go over and talk to Missis Schauble. I'll see if she has something that will calm her down. You're right! I have to do something for her first. I just don't know what to do."

Kneeling next to Molly, he lifted Emily into his arms, and whispered, "I'm sorry, Emily."

"I will go for you," Xavier offered. "You stay here with Señora Emily." Pushing himself up with his walking stick, he patted Maudie's shoulder, and hobbled through the brush toward the Schauble camp.

Some of the youngsters straggled in from searching for Amy, and then came the womenfolk. Henry Hort returned halting and bent, shaking his head. "No sign of her out there," he informed Innis. "We can't see nothing anyway," he added. "We were all milling around out there and calling for her. If she was out there, we would have heard something."

The others were nodding, as Xavier returned from the Schauble camp. Henry turned and blew his nose on the ground, one side then the other, and said, "I think you're right, Innis. She ain't lost. I think someone took her, and I think it was Comancheros."

"I'm leaving at first light," Innis announced. Then he asked Xavier, "Can you take the reins tomorrow, drive the wagon, and watch over the youngins and the womenfolk until you get them to San Felipe. Will you do that for me?"

"Of course, Señor. I am honored to do this for you." To Molly he offered a small, brown bottle and explained, "Señora Schaubel, she gives you laudanum for Señora Emily. Maybe you give this to her." Returning to Maudie, he sat and comforted her.

As Henry returned with the others to their camps, Molly administered a dose of laudanum to Emily and sat on the blanket beside her. Her heart burned with fear for Amy, and she knew there would be no sleep this night. Lying back, she gazed into the stars and waited for morning. Around the fire the refugees crawled into their bedrolls. Mothers cuddled their sick youngsters under their blankets. Xavier covered Maudie and lay next to her. As the laudanum took effect, Emily rolled onto her side and fell asleep, but for Molly the moments passed like hours.

"I got tracks over here," Innis yelled.

Molly sat up. The horizon cast a glow over Innis mounted on his horse in the brush. His grain sack of supplies hung from his pommel, and he had slung his rifle with rope over his back. Pausing to watch Molly, he assured her, "Tell Emily not to worry. I know she will anyway, but try not to. I'll catch up with you in San Felipe in two or three days."

Molly went out into the brush to beseech him. "Emily needs you here, Innis. This is crazy. Even if you find them, you can't fight them by yourself."

"I have to do this, Molly."

"I understand, but you could wait until we get to San Felipe. You could get help there. It is our capitol city, after all."

"Maybe it is, but I can't let the trail go cold. Maybe, this is the reason why I'm here, Molly. Maybe this is why I won the coin toss with Emmet. If I wasn't here, there wouldn't be anyone to go after Amy. Like you said, I might be killed, but if I'd done what I should have done and went with Emmet, I'd already be …" He stopped mid-sentence, looked down and clenched his jaw.

"What?" Molly gasped. "Dead? You were going to say that you'd already be dead, weren't you? You know this could destroy Emily."

"I can't sit back and drive that wagon like nothing happened, Molly. I can't let them get away it. There ain't no man in his right mind would do such a thing. So, you and Emily keep on going until you get to San Felipe. There's a garrison there and there's soldiers who will protect you folks. Stay with the town folks until I find you."

The brush swallowed him. The thud of his horse's hooves faded, and he was gone. Returning to the campfire, Molly glanced down at Emily, sleeping, thanks to the laudanum.

Xavier had added wood to the fire, and set over it a skillet of water and coffee. It was just starting to boil. "Buenos días," he said. "This is time for much sadness, is it not? I pray that Señor Carrigan he find little one and bring her." His voice was raspy and soft. With a small stick he stirred the roiling skillet and continued, "These days I no sleep. These days I sometimes cry too much. Men when they are old they cry too much. So, I make coffee." Pulling the skillet from the flames, he allowed the contents to settle, and asked, "You like some coffee with me?"

"Obliged," Molly replied, as she dipped a mug, and spooned up a helping of left over corn-mush from a pot hung over the fire.

Youngsters rose from their brief slumber and dashed into the bushes with their mothers and the little, sick ones, coughing and whistling. Maudie joined Xavier, rubbing her red and swollen eyes without looking up from the ground.

Shaking Emily's shoulder, Molly woke her sister, but she refused to eat after she arose, so Molly helped her up on the seat-board, and prepared to depart for San Felipe. Hitching the horses with Molly's help, Xavier cracked the reins and got the wagon under way, clattering up the drying, and now rutted and bumpy, Atascosito Road.

Emily glanced over where Innis would have been on the seat-board, and seemed surprised to see Xavier there instead. "Where's Innis?" she asked.

"He's out looking for Amy."

"Oh!" Emily's eyes glazed over, and welled up, as if she'd just recalled the horror of the night before. Into her hands she dropped her face and sobbed.

Molly gave her another dose of laudanum, and embraced her sister. Ahead, she could see Maria Benson in the back of Missis Schauble's wagon, her newborn infant under one arm, her youngest boy under the other, and he was coughing. Looking back, she could see in her own wagon three youngsters remaining out of five. Maudie's toddler and Amy were gone. Swallowing the lump in her throat, she blinked back her tears, lifted her chin, and hoped for the best. Innis might bring Amy to San Felipe. She hoped he would for Emily's sake, and hers. Holding Emily's head on her lap, she stroked her hair until she again fell asleep.

Entering bottom land that afternoon, Molly knew that it was some of the richest and most expensive farmland in Texas. Crossing one large plantation after another, she noticed that the cotton had sprouted up about six inches high. Rows of cotton stretched across expansive fields and merged into a solid mass of green in the distance. Bent over slaves hacked the ground with hoes, dozens of them. They'd rolled up their pantaloons, and their feet were bare. Their legs were soiled up to their knees, as they scraped weeds away from the cotton sprouts. Emily was awake and groggy, downcast and silent, as she also watched the toiling slaves.

That evening Molly could smell water, and knew the Brazos River was near. In the distance she could see a dogtrot beside the road. Tall pecan and twisting live oak surrounded the homestead, spreading thick canopies above. Built with logs hewn square, the dogtrot was fitted and notched together at the corners. Like two cabins facing each other, the structures were roofed together and connected with a covered platform, and an open space in between. Someone walked across the platform from one side to the other. Intrigued by the design, Molly thought it would be convenient to have food preparation separate from sleeping quarters, and have a shaded space outside to enjoy a cool breeze on hot days. A front porch, made of rived boards, spanned the full length of the combined structures, and over the porch extended a roof supported by a row of log posts and a railing.

Closer, she noticed youngsters on the porch, some down on their knees at play, others standing. Against the wall sat an adult in a rocking chair, smoking a pipe, an old woman it appeared. Some of the older youngsters and the old woman gawked silently at Molly and the town folks, as they clamored past them. She wondered if they understood the danger, which they also faced.

Beyond the dogtrot stood another homestead, and beyond that stood others. Further up, cabins lined both sides of the road. They had arrived in San Felipe. At the Brazos crossing Molly found the garrison Innis had told her about. Soldiers directed them along the riverbank into a field, where other refugees had camped. No one would be hungry tonight, for every camp they passed had a pot on the fire.

On the Atascosito by the river, Molly could see a crowded mercantile, where folks waited in line to enter. She couldn't buy anything, didn't have any money, and neither did Emily. They had to make the most of what they had. Across the street, laughter spilled from the windows and doorway of a crowded tavern. Henry Hort had parked his rig, and was already halfway there.

After supper, the womenfolk refugees gathered together at twilight to bathe in the river. Those who had shoes removed them. The others took the bandages from their feet. In turn they stood in the water, holding up blankets end to end, circling them curtain-like, behind which they proceeded with their lavations. Extending the curtain partially on shore, they provided a space for undressing and dressing, and one of the women stood back with a switch-cane to keep mischievous youngsters away. No one had soap, and the mercantile had sold out of lye for soap making. In fact, one of the women told Molly that the shelves in the mercantile were mostly bare.

Molly rinsed the grime from her hair and skin, and wrung mud from her clothing. What a relief to finally be free from the filth of the road! Emily was sullen and pale, but seemed refreshed once she'd entered the water. When she was finished, she put on one of her clean dresses, which Molly had fetched from the sea-chest, and Molly put on her lavender dress with the white brocade front and lace collar.

After sunset the camps were ablaze with crackling fires, mirth and high spirits, encouraged by the spirits obtained from across the street at the tavern. No less than six hogs were roasting on spits, most likely furnished by the good folks of San Felipe. The sound of a fiddle rose above the raucous laughter, and everyone turned to watch a lanky man strike up a tune.

"Listen," Molly grabbed Emily's arm. "He's playing that old Grumlie song we used to like."

As he played, the fiddler sang the words, and the town folks joined in:

John Grumlie swore by the light o' the moon
And the green leaves on the tree,

That he'd do more work at home a day
Than his wife could do in three.

If not distraught over Amy, Molly would have liked to join the dance. "That is one of my favorites," she said. "Come on, Emily. Let's go over and listen awhile." She lifted Emily's limp hand, and noticed that her feet would not move. Stepping in front of her, she crouched to look into Emily's downcast face, and asked, "Sister, do you feel all right?"

Emily shook her head, would not look up, and had drawn her mouth down at the corners.

"Come on." Molly reached around her waist. "I'll take you to camp and put you in bed, okay?"

The refugees had finished their supper, gathered around the fiddle player, and commenced dancing. Youngsters danced with youngsters, and boys with their mothers, while Molly made a bed of quilts upon the ground for Emily and helped her into it. It was well past sunset anyway. Then she administered another dose of laudanum. Until Emily fell asleep, Molly sat with her, listened to the fiddle player, and watched the merriment sweep the refugee's feet into motion.

"We glory … in our tribulations!" a man shouted.

Molly bolted up, surprised that the sun had suddenly risen, and didn't realize that she'd fallen asleep next to Emily. It stood to reason though. She hadn't slept for two days. On her right the sun had topped the trees, and when she turned her head, it was straight in her eyes.

The other way, she could see the man who had awakened her. Between long pauses he continued shouting. The pauses seemed to add emphasis to his words. "Knowing that tribulation worketh in us patience … and patience worketh hope … and hope maketh not ashamed …" Over at Molly he looked. She'd pushed herself to a sitting position.

Wearing a long black coat, he also wore the white collar of a clergyman, and from a leather-bound Bible he continued to read and shout his words, "In the fifth chapter of Job … we learn that man is born unto tribulation … as surely as sparks fly upward."

Molly stood up from her quilt bed, wearing yet her lavender dress. Shaking out the wrinkles, she drew a deep breath, and noticed a heavenly aroma, which made her stomach growl. Throughout the camps, pork was yet on the spit from the night before. Looking down, she noticed that Emily was still asleep.

The preacher gazed directly at her again, standing about where the fiddle player had been the night before, and surrounded by the same town folks who'd danced by the firelight. His eyes were dark and close set, separated by a long nose, and punctuated by deep scowl lines. He raised his eyebrows and his voice as he continued shouting, "But, happy is the man … whom receiveth correction … Therefore despise not your chastening … for in famine the Almighty shall redeem thee from death … and in war from the power of the sword."

"Who is he?" Molly asked one of the women, who stood beside her in the crowd.

"Eli Phipps, he's a circuit preacher," the woman informed her. "Protestants are outlawed in Texas, you know. Mexico only allows Catholics to be here, so Pastor Phipps usually holds services outdoors, or in someone's home. He comes around about once-a-month. Did y'all know it's Sunday?"

"No," Molly admitted. "I've lost track."

Pastor Eli Phipps shouted, "Is not thy wickedness great? … And, thine iniquities infinite? … Whoever perished, being innocent … or when were the righteous ever cut off?"

"What is he talking about?" Molly asked.

"What is he talking about, dear?" the woman replied with a smile. "He's talking about you. He's talking about all these folks, who's running from Santa Anna."

Molly shook her head. "These people aren't wicked, they're innocent."

The woman smiled again. "There's wickedness in all us, dear. That's why the Almighty is punishing you. That's why he's using Santa Anna to drive you out of your homes."

The preacher's voice warbled as he shouted again at the town folks, "Return to him … and thou shalt be built up … Return to him you who are rebellious and stiff-necked … and he will set up on high those that be low … and those that mourn will be exalted."

Maria Benson cried out and fell to her knees with her infant in her arms, sobbing. Others joined her, wailing their prayers and uplifting their hands to the heavens.

The woman next to Molly tugged Molly's sleeve and explained, "All you have to do, dear, is confess your wickedness. Then he will restore you, and you will prosper again."

"I refuse to do any such thing," Molly spouted. Many town folks heard her and turned their heads, and the preacher stopped shouting as Molly continued, "I haven't done anything wrong." She swung her arm around, indicating the entire crowd that surrounded her. "None of these folks have done anything wrong. They're good folks. They're the finest folks I could ever associate myself with. There's nothing they would not do for me or you, and nothing they would not share. You have no right to condemn them, Mister Eli Phipps. I won't hear any more of it." She stormed back to her wagon, even though it was only a few paces. Making an obvious display of her unwillingness to listen any longer, she knelt to awaken Emily.

Pastor Eli Phipps prayed with those who tarried, and he read further scriptures to them, and sang hymns with them. Then someone invited him to join their family for a barbeque dinner, and with that the crowd dispersed.

When Emily awoke, she picked herself up and headed straight for the bushes. While waiting for her to return, Molly ate corn-mush from a pot the refugees had hung over the fire. The intense and irresistible aroma of her neighbor's barbeque pork gnawed at her stomach. Glancing over at them, she noticed that they were already eating dinner when she had just finished breakfast.

"Would y'all like some of this?" her neighbor asked, holding up a plate of pork she had shaved from the spit.

"Oh my. Yes, I would!" And Molly hurried over to join them. As she ate, she watched Emily return from the bushes, gaunt and pale, walking slowly, carefully placing her steps one in front of the other.

"Ugh!" Emily groaned, stopped, and clasped her hands over her stomach. Turning, she ran again into the bushes.

Setting her plate aside, Molly ran after her, and assisted her sister. "Dyspepsia?" she asked.

Emily shook her head and said, "Dysentery, I think."

Helping her back into her bed by the wagon, Molly gave her another dose of laudanum and said, "I'll check around, and see if anyone has Castor Oil."

Between frequent flights to the bushes, Emily spent the rest of the day in her bed of quilts. She was not the only one with dysentery. Molly noticed that more folks than usual, both young and old, were spending excessive amounts of time in the bushes. She gave Emily Castor Oil and laudanum, which seemed to calm her and ease her peristalsis.

Innis arrived later that afternoon.

MISSIS POWELL'S TAVERN

MOLLY MUNCHED ON mesquite barbeque pork and visited with her neighbors as Innis rode into camp. Without noticing Molly, he rode right past her to Emily, who lay upon her bed of quilts.

Standing back with her neighbors, Molly allowed Innis and Emily to have their time alone, but watched them intensely for any indication of what had happened to Amy. Innis spoke with Emily, and she sat up abruptly, searching the camp, with quick, panicky glances. Molly guessed that she was looking for her, and went to her bedside.

"It's bad, isn't it?" Molly asked.

Staring down at her hands, Emily nodded.

Sitting cross-legged across from her, Innis turned his gaze to Molly, and said, "I'm sorry, Molly. Things didn't go the way I planned."

"What happened?" she asked.

"Remember when I found that trail by our wagon?"

"Yes, I remember."

"It was a good trail, and it had blood. It looked like it had been sprayed on the grass. The ground was soft and the tracks were easy to follow. I found where they tied their horses. There were others too, about five of them."

"Did you see any sign of Amy?"

"I found cloths all over everywhere. No sign of Amy though. Stuff they didn't want they just threw all over. Then they rode off. I followed them quite a ways, probably twenty or thirty miles. They had a good head start. Looked like they were riding hard most of the night maybe, four or five hours ahead of me."

"Did you see them," Molly asked. "Did you catch up to them?"

"I found one of them. I think he was the one I shot. He was a goner when I found him. Figure he must have lived an hour or so after I shot him. His buddies just left him behind. Three or four hours more and I spotted something moving in the thicket up ahead, way up ahead. Could have been wild horses, but I think it was them. They were a couple miles ahead of me and moving fast, like they knew I was following them."

"It's probably better that you didn't catch them … I mean, they might have shot you."

"Oh, I tried to catch them. I stayed on their trail until it came out on the road. It looked like they were heading down to Matagorda. There's lots of tracks on that road, Molly. I couldn't tell one set from another."

"She's lost then?" Molly's eyes began to smart. This was the outcome she'd feared most of all.

Innis continued to explain, "I wanted to go on down to the coast and hunt for them while they still had Amy, but there's islands and bays and coastline that stretch for hundreds of miles down there, maybe thousands of miles. It could take days or weeks, and I couldn't leave you here in San Felipe, waiting for me. So, I decided to come back here first. I'll take you and Emily down to Matagorda, sell our belongings, and put y'all on a ship to New Orleans. Then I'm going to search for Amy. She's my daughter, for goodness sake. I have to search for her."

Touching Emily's chin, Molly tried to get her to lift her head, but she would not look up at her. She whispered, "I'm sorry, Emily. This is all my fault. I should have stayed with you and Amy in the wagon, like Innis said that night. None of this would have happened, if I'd stayed in the wagon." Looking away, she brushed a tear from her cheek.

"Nonsense," Innis scolded her. Grasping Molly's arm, he added, "It's not your fault. If there's blame to be had, then it's mine for making camp where I did. I knew we were in dangerous country. I should have camped in a safer place, closer to the others, so we could put up a defense. I wasn't expecting something like that to happen. No one was. If you and Emily had stayed in the wagon, they would have got you, too."

Molly clenched her teeth, and spoke through them, saying, "I would have fought them, Innis, and everyone would have heard us, and they would have come running to help us."

"Maybe so, but the Comancheros most likely saw us coming before we even pulled off the road. They were waiting for us. If we hadn't gone over to help the Schaubles, they would have ambushed us. Going over there probably saved us."

"Maybe so, but it didn't save Amy, did it?"

"I'm going back down there, Molly. We'll leave in the morning. I'll comb the coast until I find her, and nothing is going to …"

The clop of horses on the Atascosito interrupted him. Hundreds of horses thundered up the road. Molly stood to watch as General Houston led his troops into San Felipe and turned in among her and the other refugees' camps along the Brazos. Horses and supply wagons passed by first, then the foot soldiers. They informed the refugees that Santa Anna was marching up the road behind them. General Houston took his troops into a pasture beyond the refugees where he had them make camp.

After their tents were pitched, and their commotion settled, Molly went into General Houston's camp to talk to the General herself. She wanted to inquire about her husband, Emmet, but an aid to the general stopped her, asking, "Can I help you, ma'am?"

"I need to speak to General Houston."

"You can see that we're at war here, ma'am. He can't be interrupted, unless it concerns the war."

"Well, it does, but mostly it concerns my husband."

"How so, ma'am?"

"He left Gonzales to join up with General Houston. I'd like to know where he is, and if he's still alive."

"I'd be happy to check the roster for you. What's his name?"

"Emmet McCracken."

"One moment."

As the aid entered the General's tent, Molly perused the troop's encampment. They'd pitched their tents in straight rows, eight perfectly straight rows with dozens of tents in each. Some of the soldiers were preparing hogs for the spit, hogs appropriated from the town folks, she guessed. Others were stacking firewood and much of the wood looked like fence posts and rails they'd pulled up from someone's field. These appeared to be truly desperate times for everyone, including the soldiers.

"Ma'am?" The aid had emerged from the general's tent. "There ain't nobody by the name McCracken on the roster. Would he have used another name?"

"No." Her heart sank to her stomach. "That's the only name he ever used. Does this mean he didn't sign up, or you just don't know where his is?"

"At the time a volunteer signs up, ma'am, their name is added to the roster. If he's deceased, we mark his name as such. If his name ain't there, then he never signed up."

Returning to camp Molly sat with Emily. She'd lost her appetite and wanted to cry, but could not. Under her quilt that night, she changed into her old, green dress, folded her lavender dress into the sea-chest, and prepared to travel the next morning.

Before daylight Innis had the horses hitched, and the wagon ready to roll. The Carrigan refugees had decided the night before to press on toward the Sabine, and then over into Louisiana. They parted company and said farewell. Innis, Emily, and Molly set out on their own and turned south on the Gotier Trace toward Matagorda.

The road was devoid of the usual teamsters who transported produce to and from the coast. Innis had the road to himself, and that made Molly uneasy for fear of an ambuscade. Frequently, Innis stopped to allow Emily to run into the bushes, followed by Molly who assisted her.

A lone wagon approached them that afternoon. The first they'd seen all day. Innis pulled into the grass alongside the road to allow it to pass. Molly expected to find the wagon loaded with freight and supplies destined for San Felipe, but instead found it loaded with furniture, household goods, and youngsters. A woman sat next to the driver, his wife most likely, and beside her sat two teenage girls. Four youngsters rode in back among the belongings.

"Y'all from Matagorda?" Molly asked.

"Yes, ma'am," the driver replied, as he pulled back his reins, and stopped his wagon. "We left two days ago, had to get out before General

Urrea gets there. He'll block the road and trap us like rats in a cage. Then he'll probably execute us like he did Commander Fannin and his men."

"What's that about Commander Fannin?" Innis asked.

"I said General Urrea will execute us like he did Fannin and his men, like he massacred them in Goliad. Y'all ain't heard about that yet?"

"No, sir."

"There was about three hundred of us with Fannin. General Urrea stood them up against a wall in the presidio at Goliad and gunned them down, just like Santa Anna did them boys at the Alamo."

The man's wife intertwined her arm with his, smiled up at him and said, "He escaped."

"You were there?" Molly gasped.

"Yes, ma'am. Me and some other boys climbed the wall and run off. See, I signed up with Commander Fannin from the beginning. He called that presidio his Fort Defiance. We all liked that, because we came to fight, and that name suited us just fine.

"Then the Garza Rancheros rose up against us, and Fannin sent about half of us out against them, and that weakened our defenses considerable. A few days after that some of our boys spotted General Urrea advancing on Fort Defiance. They could see that he was well armed with heavy cannon and a thousand or so troops. So, Fannin decided to retreat, but he kept waiting for them boys to return from the Garza Rancheros. He didn't know our boys had been whipped.

"When Urrea and his army was coming up on us, we had to pull foot. Fannin had us pile up a thousand muskets into some old rickety wagons we had, ammo in one, supplies in another, medical in another. Then he had us hitch them to a bunch of oxen we had, and hitch up our cannon, and believe me, them oxen was slower than honey in winter time. But, we headed off, and we were all pretty mad too, because we wanted to stay and fight General Urrea.

"So, the first thing that happened is the carts began to break down. They were overloaded. Then we lost some cannon when we crossed the river. Fannin made us fish them out so Urrea couldn't get his hands on them. The oxen was hungry too, and every chance they had they stopped moving and commenced to grazing.

"We had intentions of taking cover in the timber along Coleto Creek, but we was moving so slow that Urrea's cavalry overtook us. We didn't think they had the nerve to come after us, but they did. So, we hunkered down in the prairie grass behind our gear, and formed four battle lines, like a hollow square with artillery at the corners. We fought them pretty good too. We had them and their horses falling faster than they could regroup and charge at us again. I got my clothes all shot up, and lost my hat. I had a few nicks, but I didn't have any holes in me, not like the others. Even Fannin got hit a couple times in one of them volleys.

"When we got a break in the fight, we'd pick up our gear and move our battle lines closer to that timber, except for the medical wagon. The oxen pulling it was all shot up. So, we moved on without it. After that we couldn't do nothing for the wounded. I can still hear them boys crying out for help."

Pausing, the man dragged his sleeve over his eyes, and his wife threw her arms around him, as he continued, "Then we run out of water, used it up keeping the cannon cooled off, and our ammunition cart broke down. I figured we was done for about then. We couldn't run for it, and leave the wounded behind. We was all related to each other in one way or another. I had two brothers and four cousins amongst them boys myself.

"So, Fannin decided to propose terms of surrender. General Urrea listened, but wouldn't agree to it. Said he had orders, but he promised to intercede on our behalf with Santa Anna. We believed him, and we believed we was surrendering honorably, and that Mexico was going to return us to the United States. So, Urrea marched us back to the presidio and left our wounded laying out there. He forced our physicians to tend his own wounded first, and it was three days before he fetched our wounded, the ones that was still alive, that is. A bunch of us got loose one night and scrambled over the wall. I was home when I heard what happened after that. The massacre happened on Palm Sunday."

He dragged his sleeve over his eyes again, and added, "I'm getting my kin out of here, and we ain't stopping 'til we get to Louisiana."

Innis asked, "Why didn't y'all just put them on a ship?"

"There ain't no ships, mister. The Independence was ordered up to Galveston to protect the port and with the Mexican warships running all up and down the coast trying to supply Santa Anna, the freighters are afraid to come down here."

"Your losses grieve me," Molly consoled him. "I can't believe this happened again, first the Alamo, and now Goliad. That's about six hundred men we lost all together." She shook her head.

"There's a lot of folks coming up the Gotier Trace behind us," the man added. "And, they ain't letting nothing grow under their shoe leather neither, about fifteen hundred of them. So, I best be moving." He cracked his reins, and his wagon rolled ahead, toward San Felipe.

Innis turned to Emily, and asked, "What do you want to do now? There's no ships in Matagorda. Do you want to turn back? You and Molly could go back to San Felipe, and on over to Louisiana with the others. I can take my horse and go down to Matagorda and look for Amy."

Molly leaned forward to look past Emily at him, and said, "Innis, I love Amy as much as you do, and I want her back as much as you, but you're talking crazy again. You don't have a chance against a gang of Comancheros, even if you find them. And, if you run into General Urrea, you'll have no chance at all."

"I have to do this, Molly!"

"You don't have to do anything."

Baring his teeth, he snatched his hat from his head, slapped it against his thigh and said, "Y'all can't tell me what I don't have to do!"

"Well, I am, because nobody else will. Emily's sick and needs a doctor, and you want to send us off on our own. Then you want to ride off and get yourself killed. What are we supposed to do after that?"

"Stop," Emily whispered to Molly. She turned to Innis, and pulled at his sleeve with weak, pale fingers, and said, "I want Amy back. I want to go with you to find Amy. We'll go together."

Molly folded her arms and fixed her gaze on the horse in front of her. She also wanted Amy back, and said, "If going down to Matagorda is what you decide y'all want, then that's what I want, too."

Innis cracked the reins and drove along the side of the road most of the afternoon and evening, as a steady flow of wagons, pack animals, and refugees passed in the opposite direction toward San Felipe. He ate some of the pork, which folks back in San Felipe had packed for them. Emily couldn't eat, and the pork was bothering Molly's stomach. She decided she didn't want to eat any more of it. Emily hadn't eaten for a couple days, and Molly noticed that she was looking parched.

Twilight faded, and ahead they saw flickering lights where the road turned to follow the San Bernard River. Crossing a shallow creek, they followed the river until they came out in a field. At the far end Molly could see a dogtrot and several out buildings. Numerous fires dotted the area where refugees coming up from Matagorda had made camp for the night. Through the windows and doorways of the dogtrot, Molly could see a raucous crowd standing around flickering tables, and their spirits seemed high.

Innis pulled into an empty space and unhitched his horses while Molly set out to look for firewood. Emily lay on the seat-board and covered herself with a quilt.

"What in tarnation is that up yonder?" a neighbor next to them inquired, "Can y'all see that?" He pointed north, up toward the sky. "What do you suppose that is?"

Molly stopped in her tracks, and examined the familiar orange glow hanging low on the horizon. Her heart skipped. "Have mercy!" she breathed. "This can't be. All those poor folks up in San Felipe?"

Innis looked up from where he tied his horses and declared, "It's on fire. Must be a fight going on up there."

Emily climbed down from the seat-board and rushed into the bushes. Molly went after her. When they returned, the neighbor's wife and youngsters watched the horizon, and Molly noticed that many other folks had taken watch of the horizon also. To the neighbor's wife she introduced herself, and asked, "What is this place called? Where are we? Does it have a name?"

"This is Missis Powell's Tavern," she informed Molly. "The southern trails all cross here. Y'all can go anywhere in Texas from here. That building yonder is for men-folk. The other one's for womenfolk. If y'all don't have a nickel, then camping is free. Missis Powell don't never see so many folks as this. Folks say she's run out of everything. The tavern's over in that dogtrot, but they don't have nothing left to eat or drink."

Innis reached an arm around Emily's waist, pulled her to his side, and exclaimed, "Baby, it looks like there's no going back. San Felipe is on fire.

You and Molly could go to Harrisburg from here without me. There's lots of womenfolk traveling that way without their men-folk. The way things are looking you'll be safer if you ride with them. When it's over I'll come and find you."

"No," Emily whispered, and then she slipped from his grasp.

Catching her, Innis helped her stand. Molly rushed to her side, cupped her face in her hands, and asked, "You're not doing well tonight, are you?"

Emily shook her head.

"We need to build a fire and get her into bed, Innis. Can you see how she has the shakes?"

Emily clung to Molly, and Molly clung to her, as Innis built a fire and made a bed of quilts. "Okay, bring her," he said.

After putting her to bed, Molly sat with her, dozing on occasion, and rising to help when her sister needed to go to the bushes again. Emily shivered, and Molly added her own quilt to her coverings, and added wood to the fire to keep her warm.

Beside her Molly fell asleep, and before she again opened her eyes the sun had splattered its glory over the field around her. Looking over at Emily her heart filled instantly with alarm and she called out, "Innis! Come, please. Something's wrong with Emily."

RICE WATER

EMILY TRIED TO push herself up from her bed of quilts but fell onto her back. Molly tried to help her up; she slipped her arms under Emily and called to Innis, "She has to go again and I can't lift her. I need help."

Rising and shaking his head, Innis went to Emily and lifted her to her feet. Holding her against his side with one arm, he walked her to the bushes. Her head dangled and her feet didn't move much. They dragged behind her most of the way. Molly followed and was deeply troubled by what she was seeing. She'd been frightened for Amy and now she was frightened for her sister.

When Emily was finished in the bushes Molly explained to Innis, "This is twelve times she's gone since we got here last night. I'm worried she's going too much, and she's been vomiting, too."

"Has she been eating?" he asked.

"Not for three days. I'm afraid for her, Innis. Look how her eyes have sunken since yesterday and look at her hands." She held up Emily's limp hand for Innis to inspect. "Her fingers are all wrinkled up, like she's been soaking in a bath all day, but she hasn't been in the water since San Felipe three days ago when we bathed in the river."

He turned her hand in his, examining the back and then her palm. "It's just the grippe," he declared. "She'll be better by tomorrow. We can spend the day here, let her get some rest and take care of her. All of us need a rest anyways."

Emily shivered and fainted. He caught her.

"Do y'all need help?" The neighbor's wife stood on the other side of the bushes with her daughter. "I couldn't help but see you carry her over from your camp. Is she ill? Can I do anything to help?"

"Excuse me." Molly turned and ran away from them, rushing deep out-of-sight into the bushes and finding a place for her own privy. Whatever had sickened Emily seemed to be sickening her, as well. Maybe, it was the pork they had been eating. Then she remembered that Emily hadn't eaten any pork. She hadn't eaten anything.

When she returned, Innis and the neighbor and her daughter, had taken Emily to camp and covered her with quilts by the fire. Emily tried immediately to stand but fainted again. Grasping her elbows, the others kept her from falling and helped her, wobbly and faint, toward the bushes. She took only two steps before stopping to relieve herself on the ground in front of everyone. Molly was embarrassed for her but understood that she was barely able to stand, much less walk all the way to the bushes.

"My word," the neighbor's wife gasped. "I know that smell. She's all putrefied inside and she's passing rice water. I've seen this before in Charleston."

"What's rice water?" Innis asked. "We haven't seen rice since we lived in New Orleans, three or four years ago."

The woman pulled a hanky from her dress pocket and pressed it over her nose and mouth. "She's passing rice water, sir, because she's all putrefied inside."

"What do you mean?" he pondered.

"That smell," she informed him. "It's her flesh. It's got all rotten inside. I've smelled it before, and when y'all breathe that smell, that's what makes you get sick, too. Your insides will putrefy. Just like hers. Then you will die, you and your whole family. She's got the cholera, sir." The woman stepped back and grabbed her daughter's sleeve, pulling her away from Emily and saying, "We have to go."

"Wait!" Molly pleaded. "What did you do for them back in Charleston? Isn't there something we can do for her?"

The neighbor's wife backed away from Molly, holding her hanky tightly over her face and pushing her daughter toward their camp. "Well," she explained. "The doctor back there used to give them folks Castor Oil and laudanum."

"I have laudanum," Molly piped.

"You have laudanum?" The woman seemed surprised. "Then give it to her. It might help but the doctor that was giving them folks that laudanum, he was taking it too, and he got the cholera himself and died. After that we was on our own." She turned her back to Molly, and added, "We have to go."

Innis helped Emily into bed, and Molly removed her pantalets, to make it easier for her to relieve herself when she needed to. Then she gave her a dose of laudanum. Feeling weak herself, she took a seat on a blanket, leaned back on her elbows, and watched her neighbor's husband tie a shirt over his face and hitch his horses. His wife had tied a garment over her mouth and nose, as well, and threw her family's belongings from the ground into their wagon. Her small youngsters waited in line, each wearing tiny garments over their faces. Their daughter covered her mouth and hurried over to the neighbors. As they talked, the neighbors gazed at the Carrigan camp and their mouths dropped open. They, too, fetched their horses and hitched them to their wagons. Molly had seen panic before, when her own town folks evacuated Gonzales, and this was becoming a full-blown panic right before her eyes. She had to go again, stood up, and headed into the bushes.

When she returned, almost half of the overnight campers had pulled out. Many others were climbing into their wagons, but a lone woman was crossing the field and walking fast-paced toward the Carrigan camp.

Innis knelt over Emily by the fire. Molly could see that her eyes were closed, her lips were moving, and he'd turned his ear close to her.

"What's wrong?" Molly asked.

"Don't know. She's trying to say something but she isn't making sense."

The lone woman reached their camp, covered her face with a cloth, and spoke through it. "Y'all the ones that's got the cholera?" she asked.

"Yes." Molly answered.

"I'm Christiana Biladeau. My husband owns the Biladeau Cotton Works in Matagorda. I'm waiting for my family in that boarding house over yonder." She pointed across the field. "Y'all came in last night?" she asked.

"Yes, ma'am. We came in after dark. My sister here has been sick for a couple days. My brother-in-law over there thinks it's the grippe, but other folks say it's the cholera. We don't know for sure what it is. What we do know is that she's the finest person to ever walk this earth."

Emily opened her eyes and smiled up at Molly, and it was the sweetest smile that Molly could ever recall receiving from her.

"The Almighty knows." Christiana wagged her head. "He giveth and he taketh. He can give her health back. He don't take from good folks. He only takes from the wicked."

"You haven't been on the road long, have you?" Molly asked.

"I spent two days in the coach that brought me here."

"Well, we spent two weeks in the rain, the cold, and the mud. And, we buried a lot of good folks along the way. Buried them beside the road, right where they fell. You can't tell me that the Almighty doesn't take from good folks. I saw it for myself. He takes from good folks and from wicked folks alike. It doesn't make any difference. My sister's sickness is no more a sign of wickedness than her good health was a sign of goodness. We fall together, the good with the bad."

Christiana raised a finger of indictment to Molly, and said, "Then what you're saying is the Almighty is cruel."

Molly raised her finger back at her and replied, "Call it what you want. If he would listen, I would tell him we're good folks and don't deserve the things that are happening to us. I wish someone would just make him listen."

Christiana shook her finger. "Then y'all can't be the good folks you think you are. If you were, y'all wouldn't be complaining and trouble would not befall you. If you were the good folks you say, y'all would be thankful for the good things he's doing for you. And, if he isn't doing good things, then maybe y'all should be trying to find out why."

Molly lowered her finger and lifted her chin. The insult had gone straight to her heart and had left her speechless.

"I'm sorry for your misfortune," Christiana continued. "But, y'all need to move on down the road for the sake of the folks staying here. It's just common courtesy, so folks don't get infected with the cholera, or whatever else your sister's got."

Innis pursed his lips, and said, "Look ma'am. I don't care if you're Queen Biladeau from Dad-gum-gorda. My wife's too sick to be moving around. We ain't going nowhere till she gets better. So, if y'all ain't here to help us, then go on back to your boarding house and leave us be."

The woman turned and stomped back across the field, a field which was now empty, except for Molly, Innis, and Emily.

The sun rose hot that morning, and by afternoon the heat made Emily aphasic. With tree branches Innis propped up a quilt to shade her. Molly noticed that her skin had taken on a bluish-gray color. Frail and wrinkled, her skin looked old, like death. Her breath weakened, became very shallow, and then stopped altogether. Molly knew it was the end and wept for her. Innis cradled his wife in his arms, buried his face in her bosom, and heaved deep, heart-rending sobs.

Through a blur of tears Molly saw people crossing the field toward their camp. With them they carried heavy things and a woman was leading them. She had something tied over her face. They all had clothing tied over their faces. Molly blotted her tears with her dress and watched them, expecting them to run her and Innis off the field.

"I can see that one of y'all has already passed," the woman commented, as she and a group of three teenage boys gathered around the Carrigan camp. "I'm sorry for your loss. I can see that it's grieving you badly. I'm Missis Powell from the tavern. These here is my sons. We heard about your troubles and came over to help."

"Obliged." Molly introduced herself, then Innis and Emily.

"Do y'all need help burying and such?" Missis Powell asked.

"Yes, obliged."

Innis never lifted his face.

"We brought you fresh water. Figured you probably was running low on water. Our well's got the best water there ever was." Then she offered a basket to Molly. "This is the last of the cornbread. You're welcome to it. Looks like y'all need it more than we do."

"Obliged." Molly lifted the basket, and breathed in the aroma. Though she had no desire for food, she smiled, and said, "It smells good." Setting the basket beside her, she excused herself. She had to run to the bushes again.

Returning, she found Innis seated cross-legged beside Emily. Propping his elbows on his knees, he had laid his head in his hands. Shovels were shushing into the ground a few paces away, beyond the edge of the field, and they shushed their loads of soil into a great pile. Missis Powell stood by as her sons dug a grave for Emily.

Sitting with her sister, Molly watched her lifeless body intently, recalling how they had grown up together and loved each other. Running all their joyful events through her mind, she realized that those memories were now her most cherished possession.

Emily appeared to be bloating. Molly suspected that it was the heat, and noticed that her body was swelling quickly. Her face wasn't the face of her sister anymore, but had become the face of some strange puffy person. The color that had tinted her skin had deepened to blue-gray until she no longer looked human. Molly reached to touch her, but a loud hissing sound caused her to withdraw her hand, and the heavy smell of fetid flesh filled her nostrils and the air around her, gagging her, and stopping her breath. She turned and retched in the grass, retched until she thought her insides would burst open.

Innis lifted his swollen eyes to her, and asked, "You have any of that laudanum left?"

She answered, as she faced the ground, "Yes, about half of it."

"Y'all better start taking some yourself then. You're not looking too good Molly. You look about the same as she did yesterday."

"I don't think I can do anything right now."

"Where is it? I'll get it for you."

"I put it in the sea-chest."

From the chest he brought the tiny bottle, pulling the cork and handing it to her, he said, "It's bad losing Emily. I don't want to lose you, too. Take it for Emily. She'd want you to take it, Molly. And, take it for Amy. She's going to need you when I bring her back."

Molly took the laudanum and returned the bottle to him.

The shushing stopped. Missis Powell approached and informed them, "We're ready for her." Her sons carried Emily by the corners of the quilt she lay on, and they lowered her, folding the sides over her and covering her completely.

Missis Powell bowed her head. Everyone bowed their heads and Molly began to weep again as Missis Powell prayed, "Lord, we don't know why you've called this youngster of yours home but we know she's safe in your hands. We know they're good hands, too, and we know you'll take good care of her. We understand that nothing that belongs to the earth is allowed to leave the earth, and that's why we are placing her body here in the earth today. The most important part of her is the part that belongs to you, and we're thankful because that part of her is with you right now. Without knowing that we wouldn't none of us have no hope at all. Amen."

The boys said, "Amen."

Molly couldn't speak. Staggering to the campfire, she fell upon her quilt, rolled onto her back, and drifted off to a place she had known once before, in a time when life was joyful and good. Emily was there with her and she was showing her a new twisting stitch that she used for making tatted buttons. A cool breeze was blowing through the window and lifting the curtains. A voice came through the window, a shushing sound like the wind.

Shush.

She heard the sound, and her eyes opened. Her vision came slowly into focus and she noticed that her skin felt hot and dry. She lifted her hand and saw the deep folds that creased her fingers, like she'd been bathing all day. Turning her head she could see blades of grass standing like trees around her.

Shush.

She heard the sound again and it frightened her. She realized that she had to go to the bushes right away and tried to lift herself, but could not. Propping herself on one elbow, she could see Innis. He had a shovel and he was digging next to Emily's grave.

Shush.

He tossed another load of soil into a pile.

Over Emily's grave stood a cross made of tree branches and tied together. He might have carved something on it, but it was too far away to see clearly.

Innis. Her mouth formed his name, but no sound came out from her, and her elbow refused to hold her up any longer. She slipped onto her back. It was then she realized that Innis was digging another grave and it was for her.

SUGAR LEAD

SHE RECOGNIZED THE smell. It was the same smell Emily had, and Molly noticed that it now came from within herself. Her insides had putrefied. That's what the neighbor had said would happen. She said her insides would putrefy and then the whole family would die. Innis would be next. Molly wanted to cry, but her tears withered within her hot, dry eyes.

For a moment she was glad that the Comancheros had stolen Amy. At least she would have a chance to survive. Molly's chance was slipping rapidly away from her. Amy hadn't been exposed to this putrefying disease. The Comancheros had saved her from that. Who would have suspected something good would come from such a catastrophe, and if Amy ended up someplace even remotely decent, she might have a chance at a good life. Molly hoped so for Amy's sake. She prayed that she would have a good life. No one else could help her now.

Opening her eyes, she found that the sky was clear and sunny, but the quilted canopy above no longer shaded her. The sun had moved and drove its horrid heat into her bones and puckered her skin.

Her tongue cleaved to the roof of her mouth as she tried again to call Innis, his shovel shushing soil repetitiously. She couldn't speak and with great exigency needed to go to the bushes. She refused to relieve herself where she lay and would rather die.

From her quilt she rolled onto her elbows, dragged herself into the grass, and relieved herself there. The cramps were less intense. She thanked the laudanum for that, but she was thirsty, so very, very thirsty. She thought that her thirst alone would kill her.

Missis Powell's sons had brought them water, she recalled. The best water there ever was. On the other side of her quilt she could see the bucket they had brought. To it she pulled herself, and it seemed to take hours to crawl all the way over there. A blur stood over her. She realized that it was Innis, and he was holding something in his hand, a dipper. He held it for her as he boosted her up. From the dipper she drank, crystal clear, cool and sweet water, delightful as it loosened her tongue, washing the dryness from her mouth into her stomach.

"Thank goodness!" he said, and dragged his sleeve across his eyes. "I couldn't wake you up, Molly. Thought I was going to lose you just like that. I'm really glad you woke up."

The water did not stay in her stomach for long. She turned her head and retched. Then she drank again, drank until her stomach was full. Innis carried her back to her bed, and adjusted the overhead quilt-canopy to give her shade.

"Here." He pulled the cork from the tiny bottle of laudanum. "Take some more of this. It seems to be helping. Missis Powell was here again. She's worried about you, too. She gave me some kind of sugar-powder. Said to put it in your water and I drank some, too."

Again she slept, as the laudanum took full effect. When she awoke, she found herself in a dark room. Across the room a small fire flickered in a stick and mud chimney. Dawn had broken over the tree tops at the edge of the field and rays of sunlight sliced through the open window above her bed. A cool breeze drifted in. On the floor next to her Innis sat cross-legged with his back against a wall of squared logs. His head hung in front of him, fast asleep. She tried to roll on her side, but couldn't move very much.

Innis lifted his head, his eyes swollen, but not as red as the day before. "You're awake," he muttered. "Good. That's good. Missis Powell says I need to get you to drink lots of water. Are you thirsty?" he asked.

She nodded.

Helping her to a sitting position, he offered her a dipper of water. When she was satisfied, he gave her two more drops of laudanum. "I put some more of that sugar powder in your water," he explained. "Missis

Powell wanted me to bring you over here. We're inside her house. She thinks if you make it through the day today, you'll probably get better. The boarders are afraid of you, and they put up a fuss, but she said it wasn't none of their business who stayed in her side of the dogtrot. She said if they didn't like it, they could just pack up and leave. I'm kind of liking Missis Powell … She prayed for you last night. I don't take much to praying and such, but I have to admit you are looking better today, and I'm really glad you woke up this morning."

Molly slept most of the day, awaking in the evening. She realized that she hadn't needed to go to the bushes since the day before, and she was hungry. Innis gave her water, the last of the cornbread, and laudanum. Then she slept again until the next morning.

Innis was not in the room when she awoke, but Missis Powell stood in front of the chimney, adding wood to the fire. "Morning," she said. "Innis and my boys are outside dressing a hog. They found an old sow rooting around back in the woods. Don't know who it belongs to. Don't matter much anyways. Everyone's skedaddled for Louisiana. Them boys are going to bone out that old sow and we'll roast it right here in the hearth. I got to build up a bed of coals for roasting, and I'm throwing in a little mesquite for flavor … Are you feeling better?"

"Yes," Molly replied, and pushed herself up on one elbow.

"Willikers," Missis Powell said. "That's the first thing I heard out of you in three days."

"I need to go, Missis Powell."

"I'll help you." She lay her wood aside and helped Molly out of bed, as she observed, "Your skin is starting to plump up again. You were looking powerful bad the last couple days." She pulled Molly's arm over her shoulder, and reached around her waist. Out behind the dogtrot she led her to a privy, which the boarding house guests had been using. She explained, "Go on inside, and if y'all need help, just say so."

She continued talking after closing the door and it muffled her voice. "You're so thin now. I don't know how much you lost, but it looks to me like half of you is gone. I was hoping I could roast that sow and get y'all to eat some of it. That would help put some meat back on your bones. If you think you're up to eating some of it, that is."

Three days passed before Molly could get herself out of bed and walk to the privy without assistance. When she was able, Missis Powell heated water for her to take a bath. She filled a watering trough behind the dogtrot, one that she rented to the boarders for bathing.

"You're a lucky girl," Missis Powell kept saying as she pulled a curtain around Molly and helped her into the trough. "But you're so skinny. Would y'all like me to take in that dress of yours so it fits better after I wash it for you?"

"Obliged," Molly thanked her, as she reclined in the luxurious heated water. "There is one thing I need to do though," she added, "if you might be willing to help me."

"Glad to do what I can."

"Do y'all have a fixative like salt or vinegar?"

"We've never had vinegar here. Suppose we would if the spirits I keep for the tavern ever turns bad, but the spirits don't never last long enough to turn bad around here. We get some folks that turn pretty bad themselves from time to time though." At her own joke she laughed and her belly jiggled. Then she frowned. "The food and the spirits is gone. All used up. Thank heaven for that hog your brother-in-law got or we'd be starving right now. There's no salt neither. Used that all up, too, but I got acetate of lead. That's what I've been using for a fixative when I needs it, which ain't often. Bought a big bag of it from them traders one time when they was passing through, a five pounder. And that's what I give folks when they come down with the grippe. Had a doctor stay here one time and he told me about its medicinal uses. So, I give it to them in a cup of water. They call it sugar lead. I gave some to your brother-in-law to give to you when I saw how sick you were and I've been putting it in your water since he brought you over here. Even took some myself, just in case. I mostly use it for fixing dye. You see, I don't like to use the chamber lye as a fixative. I save that for the privy. If I run out of chamber lye the privy will stink to high heaven. I bought the acetate of lead so I wouldn't have to use chamber lye. Never figured I'd use it for fixing up sick folks too." She belly laughed again. "You want to dye something?" she asked.

"I would like to wear a mourning dress in memory of my sister," Molly replied weakly, "but I'll need to dye my good dress first."

"I understand." Missis Powell nodded. "Then y'all will be needing blood-wood too. That's hard to come by in these parts, but I got some. You can see by the dress I'm wearing that I'm partial to black, so I keep blood wood shavings for dyeing my clothes. You're welcome to what's left, in memory of your sister."

"You are more than kind to me, Missis Powell. I'm beholding to you."

In her own hearth, Missis Powell helped Molly boil shavings to make black dye. Molly stirred in her lavender dress, the one with the white brocade front and lace collar, which Emily had stitched in. The white front didn't take the dye as well as the lavender fabric, so she boiled it again until it was suitably black, and then simmered it in a solution of acetate of lead to set the color. By midday it was laundered and drying in the sun. Then Molly slipped it on.

"My goodness." Missis Powell stood back, hands akimbo, and smiling. "We need to take this one in a mite, too. I can do it now, if you like."

Wearing her freshly dyed and freshly tailored black dress, Molly started out across the field toward Emily's grave. As she approached she recalled how her mother had mourned when her father passed. Her mother had dyed one of her dresses and she would have dyed a dress to mourn for Emily, too, if she were yet alive. It seemed proper that Molly would keep the tradition and carry the burden of mourning for her beloved sister in that way. Her steps were long and arduous, exhausting her in her weakened condition.

Innis saw her and dashed across the field after her. Alongside, he hooked his elbow in hers and said, "It's nice to see you up." He gave her a smile of genuine relief and inquired, "You need help with anything?"

"I want to pay my respects to Emily. I might not ever come back here again."

They reached the mound where Innis had fashioned a cross and next to Emily's mound Molly saw an unmarked mound.

"Don't pay no attention to that one." Innis indicated the unmarked mound. "Wait a minute." He sprang into the brush and disappeared.

While he was gone, Molly traced the letters of Emily's name with her fingers where Innis had carved them into the arm of the cross. At the base lay a bouquet of flowers, withered and brown, crumbling when she knelt to touch them. Standing again, she fixed her eyes on the dried flowers.

When he returned, Innis held out to her a fresh bouquet of bluebells, orange paintbrush, and pink primrose. With long strands of wild grass he had bound the stems together and tied them. "These were her favorites," he explained. "I thought you'd like to give them to her."

Silently, she knelt, and laid the fresh flowers next to the dry ones. "I never stop thinking about her," she whispered.

"Neither do I," he added.

"I carry her right here." Molly placed her fist over her heart, "inside me."

"So do I."

"What are we going to do?"

"Well, Molly, we haven't had a chance to talk about this. We need to talk about it. We can't stay here much longer. It's too dangerous."

"I know."

"We have to make a choice. We can head east to Harrisburg if you like."

Molly didn't take her eyes from the flowers, as she whispered, "I want to find Amy."

"There's not much chance of finding her now, Molly. It would be dangerous, too, more dangerous than staying here."

"I know, Innis, but I feel like I'm standing on the edge of a cliff, and I'm waving my arms to keep my balance, to keep from falling off. There's nothing below, just emptiness. I don't care about anything else. Nothing else seems important. Emily wanted to search for Amy down in Matagorda, and now that's what I want to do for her. I don't care what happens to me. I have to try and find Amy for Emily's sake. It was her last wish. Can you understand that?"

"Yes. That's been my same feeling all along."

Molly turned to him. "Then let's go."

"Now? You want to leave now?"

"Why not now? There's nothing for us here."

"We only got five or six hours of daylight left today."

"How far would that get us?"

"Maybe, ten miles."

"Then that's ten miles closer to Amy than we are now."

Molly returned to the dogtrot, changed out of her black dress, and explained her intentions to Missis Powell. Understanding the weightiness of present circumstances and the threat of General Urrea's approach, she did not oppose Molly; she rather encouraged her. "I don't know what y'all will find down in Matagorda," Missis Powell advised her, "but I pray y'all will find your little niece, and I hope that's all you find."

"Obliged, Missis Powel, you saved my life, you know."

"Not me. It was one much greater than me what done it."

While Innis hitched the horses Molly said her goodbyes, and outside she could hear the wagon clatter up to the dogtrot and stop. Giving Missis Powell a quick embrace, she rushed out, climbed up on the seat-board, and departed with him on short notice.

At the crossroads Innis pulled back on the reins, stopped the wagon, and examined the road to Harrisburg. There was no afternoon breeze. Blistering hot, the air had also become dead calm. Molly couldn't see anyone traveling the roads in any direction. Even the birds had taken to shade, and the crickets had fallen ominously silent. A chill ran up her spine in spite of the heat.

Lowering his gaze and pushing back his hat, Innis asked, "You sure you want to do this, Molly?"

"I'm sure."

Cracking the reins, he drove the wagon with a lurch south onto the Gotier Trace toward Matagorda. That night he pulled off the road beside a creek, next to a thicket, unhitched and watered the horses. Molly noticed that the air was hotter and deader than when they left Missis Powell's Tavern.

Prickly ash, hackberry, and green briar clogged the thicket and were tangled together with rattan and other vines, which made the gathering of firewood difficult but not impossible. Innis went out to hunt for supper as Molly searched the sea-chest for her leather gloves, which she had made back home. For meat processing and berry picking she had also made a leather apron, but didn't know what happened to the gloves or the apron. Pushing her way into the thicket, she collected wood for a fire.

As dry branches cracked beneath the bindings around her rotten shoes, she recalled how she and Emily would pick blackberries, dewberries and mulberries in the spring. They could hardly move in the thickets around Gonzales and knew it would hurt when they did; but the pies, which came with berry picking, made the effort worthwhile.

Stacking deadwood by the wagon, she proceeded to clear a place for a fire. Innis returned with an armadillo skewered on a pitchfork. Sweat ringed the neck of his shirt, as he held it up and smiled. When it was cooked, Molly was surprised by how much it tasted like pork. He claimed that he had eaten armadillo before, but she wasn't sure she believed him, thinking that he was only interested in getting her to eat something, anything.

The next morning was cool, but the second day grew hotter than the day before. On the third day they rose before dawn, leaving early to take advantage of cooler morning temperatures. Molly watched the road come into view as the sun rose. The lazy clop of their horses and the clatter of the wagon wheels gave her a sense of well being.

A band of blue clouds rested on the horizon. At least she thought they were clouds, and then realized it was Matagorda Bay she was looking at, shimmering distant and brilliant. Estimating that they were ten or twenty miles from Matagorda, and beyond that the bay, she was amazed by its great expanse, and how the bay looked very much like part of the sky before her.

Drawing a deep breath, she captured the sweet fragrance of spring, and watched as sunlight revealed patchy thickets covered with blossoms of magenta, ocher, and blue. "It looks like those stumps up there are moving," she observed. "Are they moving, Innis?"

"I don't think they're stumps, Molly." Innis reached behind the backboard and drew his rifle from its scabbard. "I was afraid of something like this. I wish we had another rifle. Get that pitchfork back there and hurry. Arm yourself with it, Molly, and do it like you mean it."

A clench of nausea gripped her stomach. She jolted around and climbed over the backboard, took up the pitchfork, and prepared to thrust it into anyone who approached them from the road. What she thought were stumps emerged from the shadows, walking up the side of Gotier Trace toward their wagon, three of them, bare to the waist. Their skin was dark, almost black. Leather flaps covered their loins, and they wore leggings of leather and moccasins. Bushy and dirty, their hair was not combed or braided like other natives she'd seen. Their tribe was not evident in their appearance, Comanche, maybe, and part Spanish. Her pulse throbbed in her neck and in her temples. Her vision swooned and her surroundings darkened, except for those three natives.

One of them made signs to Innis with his hands, as the other two continued along the side of the wagon where Molly stood. Light headed and faint, she brandished her pitchfork and held her breath.

One with a disfigured face had a scar extending down his forehead and through his nose. As he approached, she noticed that the bridge of his nose was flat with his cheeks. Only the tip and nostrils protruded and he appeared to be proud of his disfigurement, for he had tattooed his face blue and black to make the massive scar stand out. At the back of his head he'd pulled his hair, tying it into a plume. Disregarding her pitchfork, he looked over the sideboard, and seemed to take inventory of the possessions stacked at Molly's feet.

The third native had evil, coal-black eyes, and moved past the disfigured native toward the back of the wagon. Bushy hair and a pointed beard covered most of his face. Though his clothing was like the Comanche, she could tell that he had mostly Spanish blood in his veins. Against him she raised her pitchfork and gasped.

With his back to her, Innis stood and raised his rifle, cocking it. The click of the firing mechanism seemed to be a threat, which the natives understood.

Glancing at Innis, and back to the one at the rear, Molly determined that she would not show fear, but knew it was exuding from every part of her body. Forcing herself to be calm, her eyes met those of the evil-eyed native with the bushy hair and pointed beard. His coal-black eyes sent a chill up her spine, for they were filled with loathing and hate. Her arms and legs became loose and shaky as she watched him rummage through the belongings at the rear of the wagon.

The disfigured native said something in Spanish. Then the evil-eyed native spat and turned away. The native in front completed his sign language with Innis and joined the others. Together the three of them continued walking up Gotier Trace.

"Land sakes alive!" Innis exclaimed. Lowering his rifle, he lifted his hat, and dragged perspiration from his brow with the back of his hand.

Molly laid her pitchfork in the wagon, slumped down behind the back-board, and held back her tears.

"You alright?" he asked. "You did good, Molly. They weren't armed, so I wasn't too worried. I just hope that's the last we see of them."

"What did they want?"

"My horse. They saw my horse tied to the back of the wagon and wanted to buy it. They claimed that they had gold. You know that we ain't going to find more horses in Matagorda. No matter how much gold we got. There ain't no horses anywhere. That's why they wanted to buy ours. Gold ain't good for nothing, if there ain't nothing to buy. So, I bet now they're going to try and steal our horses."

"I don't know if this is worth it, Innis. They frightened me."

"I was ready for them. Sometimes I think you don't really know what I'm capable of, even after all this time."

"I know what you're capable of, Innis." Wiping perspiration from her own forehead, she also pressed her fingers against her temples to ease the throbbing there, and she said, "Sometimes I don't know what I think. Did you hear the native speaking in Spanish?"

Lifting his brow, Innis asked "The one with the scarred face?"

"Yes."

"I thought I heard him speaking Spanish, but I was so fixed on that one in front of me … You know, Molly, I think I've seen the one with the scarred face before, back in Gonzales. You can't never forget a face like that. He was passing through and tried to buy a rifle at the mercantile. Mister Schauble wouldn't sell it to him. If it's who I think it is, he's nothing but a thieving, no good Comanchero. Folks have even sent Rangers out after him and that bushy-haired one he's running with. They're Comancheros. I'm sure of it, Molly. We could be in trouble here."

As if she wasn't frightened enough already, the prospect of Comancheros finding her and Innis before they could find Amy terrified her. She climbed over the backboard to face him, and asked, "What should we do?"

"I think they were just looking us over to see what we got and see how we're armed. There's probably more of them somewhere. I think we better unhitch the horses." His voice became low and urgent as he continued, "We can make a run for it, leave the wagon behind. Maybe, that will keep them occupied long enough for us to get to Matagorda."

"What about all our things, Emily's loom and her spinning wheel?"

"We can get more things, Molly."

"But, they're Emily's things!"

"They can't outrun our horses, Molly, but they can sure enough outrun our wagon. Which do you want?"

She agreed, and he climbed down to unhitch the horses. Saddling his own horse, he tied his supply sack to the pommel, and suggested, "You ride my horse with the saddle. I'll ride one of these other horses bareback." Re-attaching the rope-sling to his rifle, he hung it over his back.

"I want that pitchfork," Molly insisted. "I saw what you did to that armadillo with it."

Fashioning another sling from a piece of rope, he attached it to the pitchfork, and hung it over Molly's back with the tines sticking up behind her head. They left their belongings behind, mounted up and kicked their horses toward Matagorda, tagging the third horse along as a spare.

Riding dried the perspiration under Molly's clothing, and gave her a sense of release from her worries. Further they rode, until the land became a grassy, coastal plain, devoid of trees. Before the sun had peaked, she could see a few trees and buildings in the distance. It was Matagorda. She and Innis slowed to a canter when they entered the main street.

Doors and windows stood open, and the wind flapped a shutter back and forth, as if banging a dirge. Broken crates, furniture, and clothing littered the street. Shops, boarding houses, and taverns were empty. Down the street they made their way until it ended at Matagorda Bay.

As they neared the water's edge, Molly pointed into the Bay, and said, "Look Innis. There's a ship out there." It was misty, but in full view, a triple master with gun ports along its sides. "I see people out there," she added, as she noticed a keelboat loaded with wooden crates, and manned by a crew of oarsmen. The boat was about halfway to shore.

Pulling up when they reached the end of the street, Molly noticed the Biladeau Cotton Works on the west, a large, plank and beam building overlooking the bay. The full length of the building was spanned by a loading dock, which faced the street. Backed up to the dock was a large freight wagon. Three men busily stacked crates and barrels in the wagon. Bare to the waist, they paused to watch Molly and Innis, mostly watching Molly.

"Hello!" Innis raised his hand to greet them. "Y'all live here in Matagorda?"

The laborers set down their crates, looked at each other, and laughed. "No comprendemos Inglés, señor." They laughed again and spoke to each other in Spanish. One of them dashed into the building.

From the Biladeau Cotton Works emerged a rotund man onto the loading dock, wearing a broad sombrero. His shirt was neatly tucked behind a red sash, which girded his waist and hung at his side. Under the sash Molly could see the butt of a dueling pistol, and the man had placed his hand upon it.

MATAGORDA

"LET'S WAIT RIGHT here." Innis pulled his reins to the side, and turned his horse to face the loading dock. Beside him, Molly also turned as he mumbled, "Better we stay here out of range of that pea shooter of his."

"What is it you are looking for, señor," the rotund man hollered.

"We're looking for folks here in Matagorda that, maybe, can help us find my daughter, sir."

"Your daughter, señor?"

"Yes, she's three years old. Her name is Amy and she has light blonde hair. Have you seen or heard of a little girl like that?"

"No, señor. I do not know little girl. Someone I know can help you. I can take you, and they will help you. You and your wife come with me, and I show you."

"My wife?" Innis glanced at Molly and smiled, then hollered, "Yes! Yes, my wife. We'll tie our horses, and be right with you."

"Sí, you go. Tie horses. Then you come, and I will show you who will help you find little girl."

Innis nudged his horse alongside the Biladeau Cotton Works, dismounted and tied it to a rail. Molly also dismounted.

"I don't like this, Innis," she cautioned him.

"Why not?" he asked.

"They don't belong here. Those men. This just doesn't feel right to me. And, that man, he isn't Mister Biladeau. I don't think Mister Biladeau is Spanish."

"They're making me a mite nervous, too," he admitted. Slipping the rifle from his back, he checked the primer, and laid the weapon over his forearm. "What else can we do?" he asked, as he untied his supply sack and slung it over his shoulder.

She pulled the pitchfork from over her shoulder, held it in both hands before her, and said, "Why don't we keep going, just get away from here?"

"Where will we go?" Innis asked. "Do we go into the sea? This is the end of the road, Molly. We can't swim for it, and we can't run back to the wagon and the Comancheros."

She shook her head. "I don't trust those men, the way they were looking at me. I'm glad you let them think I was your wife. Maybe, they'll leave me alone."

"I'm telling you, Molly, you worry too much. They're not going to bother you. I sure enough wouldn't bother a woman with a pitchfork. They're smart enough to know better, too."

Molly didn't reply.

"Besides," he added. "If someone tries to shoot you, most likely they'll miss. It ain't as easy as you think to shoot someone, especially if they're moving. If you're close enough to stick them with that pitchfork, you ain't going to miss. That's a fact, and they'll be plenty surprised when you do it, too.

"Are you up to this, or not, Molly? You said it didn't matter what happens after we get here. Are you going through with it or not? If you're changing your mind, just tell me now. I'm willing to make a run for it, but I don't think there's anywhere to run. We might make it past the Comanchero's, and get back to Missis Powell's, but then we'll have to face General Urrea. So, what's it going to be?"

She fixed her gaze on the loading dock and the men who waited there. Narrowing her eyes, she tightened her grip on her pitchfork, and nodded, saying, "I'm up to it."

Innis suggested, "First, let's go and find out who he wants us to talk to."

Returning to the loading dock, Molly could see that the keelboat had landed, and the laborers had joined the oarsmen. Unloading the cargo, they carried crates to the dock, and stacked them near the freight wagon, which was already full. Waiting on the ground below the loading dock, was the rotund man.

On his hips he rested his hands. He was smiling, not a warm smile, but one which suggested he might have smelled something bad. When they were close enough, he offered his hand to Innis, and introduced himself, "I am Alejandro Dionisio de Zsohar, the alcalde of Matagorda."

"The mayor?" Innis asked.

"Sí!"

Innis introduced himself and introduced Molly as his wife. He explained the abduction of Amy, and why they'd come to Matagorda, and then asked, "Why haven't you run off to Louisiana with the rest of the Matagorda folks?"

"I am appointed alcalde by the government of México to oversee Matagorda. I have to fear nothing from México. I stay here. Thees is my home. There are many who make thees their home too. They stay here, too. I am their alcalde."

"Who's cargo is that on the dock?" Innis asked.

"Thees?" the alcalde squeaked, turning and waving his upturned palm from the keelboat to the loading dock. "Thees belong to Señor Sam Houston. We take to him. And, thees ship." He pointed to the misty ship in Matagorda Bay. "It is the ship called Independence. It belong to Tejas navy. Señor Sam Houston is sending thees ship to Galveston. Today it leaves, and we take cargo to him." Again the alcalde placed his hands on his hips. "Now we go talk to one who can help you find little girl." Up the street he began to walk. "Come! We go now!"

Innis turned to follow him.

Molly grabbed his sleeve. "Innis!" she whispered. "He's lying. Can't you tell he's lying?"

"Do we have a choice?" he asked.

"Yes," she insisted. "Make him bring them to us."

Innis stopped in his tracks. "Sir! Mister Alcalde!" he called.

In the middle of the street the alcalde turned and faced them, smiling. "Something, Señor Carrigan?"

"Can you bring them out here to talk to us?"

"Of course. Wait here. Momento, por favor." The alcalde hurried across the street and entered one of the vacant-looking buildings, crouching to enter a low doorway.

Molly tugged on Innis's sleeve again, and said, "Let's get off the street. Okay?"

Hooking her arm, Innis went back the way they'd come, toward the Biladeau Cotton Works. It was then that Molly heard the click of a rifle cocking.

"Run!" Innis huffed, and sprinted with her arm hooked in his.

Alongside him she sprinted with surprising ease in spite of her rotten shoes. Until now she hadn't realized how much swifter she was on her feet than Innis. Together they leapt, and tumbled behind the cover of a broken crate. Innis fell on his rifle, and Molly fell on her pitchfork. Fortunately, the tines were pointing away from her. Up the street, Innis watched where the alcalde had gone, and Molly looked back toward the loading dock.

"Innis, look!" She indicated the loading dock.

The laborers were hitching a team of horses to the freight wagon. One of them stood behind the horses and in front of the wagon. Laughing and lifting the kingpin, which attached the horse's rigging to the tongue of the wagon, he waited until Innis was looking at him and then dropped the kingpin into place with a click. The laborers pointed at Molly and Innis and laughed long and hard at them.

"Americano," one of them hollered. "You are too much like the mouse. You are afraid of everything."

Behind them a voice said, "Thees is my brother, Padre Zsohar."

Molly and Innis spun around to see the alcalde standing in the street with a man about his own age wearing a black cassock.

"He lives in back over there." The alcalde indicated the building he had entered and emerged from. "He will help you."

The padre lifted his face to look at them, a chiseled face that bore the scars of battle. He made the sign of the cross and his eyes could not hide the kindness within him. Innis lifted his hand, and the padre took it in both of his. In a soft voice he said, "My brother Alejandro says you need to speak with me. Come to my church, you and your wife, and together we will speak. There I will help you, my son. Do not be afraid."

From the main street Padre Zsohar led them, as the alcalde watched, smiling, with his hands on his hips. Onto a side street they turned. Tiny homes lined the side street. Built of rived boards and some adobe, the homes were covered with shake roofs. A hitching rail marked the end of the street, and beyond the rail stood a whitewashed church. Overshadowing the church was a cross, which stood on the ridge board above the doors. The padre pulled a ring attached to one of the heavy, rough-sawn double doors, and opened the sanctuary.

Molly entered first, and then Innis, followed by the padre. Inside, Molly could smell earth, like a freshly plowed field. At the side of the sanctuary the padre unlatched and opened a shutter, which held back the sun. Light spilled across the earthen floor, and Molly noticed that the sanctuary was large enough for, maybe, a hundred people to stand together. At the far corner, three steps led up to a raised pulpit. In the corner, opposite the pulpit, the padre opened a door to a small side room.

"Come," he said, and waved them in. He unlatched and opened a smaller shutter and sunlight illuminated the little room. He indicated that they should take seats upon a bench, and next to them he took a seat behind a lattice partition, which divided the bench and separated them. "What is it that you would like to confess?" he asked.

"What do you mean confess?" Innis asked, visibly taken back. Molly perceived his surprise from the expression on his face, as he informed the padre, "I'm trying to find my daughter."

"I am here to listen, my son. What would you like to tell me?"

Innis raised his voice, "First of all, I'm not your son. Second, the alcalde told us you would help us find my daughter. And third, I ain't here to confess nothing. I ain't done nothing I should have to confess for."

"We all must confess, my son. Then I will help you." The padre's voice remained soft and calm, as he added, "We all fall short."

"I ain't confessing!" Innis bellowed. "I don't believe …"

Molly stopped him by laying her hand on his, and saying, "Let me! Please!" She directed her response to the padre, and made the sign of the cross. "My last confession was four years ago."

"Do you trust the Almighty?" the padre asked.

"Yes, I trusted him once. I trusted him until he let the war take away our farm and everything we've worked for the past four years. I trusted him until he let the Comancheros take Amy, and then he let the cholera take my sister, and let it almost take me. Sometimes I wish that it had taken me, Padre. The cholera would have spared me the sorrow that I now have to live with. My sister has gone to a place where there is no sorrow. Why couldn't I have gone there with her?" Molly buried her face in her hands.

The padre replied through the lattice, "I see that you are angry with the Almighty."

"Yes! I'm angry, Padre. Why is he doing this? I want to know why he isn't helping us. I want him to answer me."

"Because, my child, his ways are above our ways. His foolishness is wiser than our wisdom, and his weakness is greater than our strength."

"Foolishness!" Molly glared at him. "Is that what did this to us, his foolishness?"

"And now, you would mock him?" the padre asked.

"Mock him? No! I would never mock him. I'd rather die than mock him."

"Then you say that you would honor him with your very life, but you are angry with him? You accuse him?"

"Of not doing anything when he could have helped us? I suppose I am accusing him of that. Yes!"

"And, if you perceive that he is not doing anything for you, this seems unjust to you?"

"Not only is it unjust, Padre, it's unfair. It's not right. I trusted him, and he did this to us, to our family, to Emily, and to me."

"You must begin to trust him again before you can confess."

"I don't know if I can, Padre. I haven't done anything to deserve this. At least I can't think of anything I've done to deserve it. Unless it's something I did when I was growing up. I can't remember."

The padre explained, "Many are unaware that they are full with the mistakes of their youth. They follow selfish desires and vain ambitions from the time that they are small children. When they are old, they go into the land of others and drive out the rightful tenants and call it their own land, taking what is not theirs to take. They build houses of stone and wood and cultivate fields of hay and straw for their cattle. From those who have not, they gather, and to those who have need, they give nothing. Their slaves they beat down until their slaves return to the dust from which they were made, and then they call themselves judicious. To them, all mankind is lowly when their skin is not white like their own. To them, the purpose of us who have dark skin is to carry their burdens and provide for their comfort. Upon the backs of the poor they build their empires, and to no one do they give an answer for what they have done. But, one day they will be made to answer. One day they will be made to repay in full what they have taken. Even now they are paying for what they have done."

"You mean what I have done, don't you?" Molly asked.

"That is why you are weak and sickly, my child."

Innis jumped to his feet, clenching both of his hands into fists. Molly placed her hand upon one of them, and said, "It's all right, Innis. He isn't going to help us. I think we should leave. We should go sell our horses and see if we can buy passage on the Independence before it leaves Matagorda Bay."

"The Independence?" the Padre asked, as he too stood. Together he folded his hands, interlaced his fingers and added, "The Independence left Matagorda last month. You have come too late to obtain passage on the Independence."

"Last Month?" Molly gasped, and sprang to her feet. "I knew he was lying, Innis. The alcalde lied to us about that ship." The padre's eyes became noticeably large, and Molly bared her teeth at him, asking, "It's a Mexican warship, isn't it? That ship is Mexican, and its bringing supplies for Santa Anna, isn't it?"

Innis grabbed her hand. "Come on. Let's get out of here."

Together they dashed from the church and up the street. Turning the corner, they ran toward the Biladeau Cotton Works. When they reached the hitching rail, they discovered that their horses were gone. At the loading dock they saw no one. The freight wagon was gone, so were the laborers, and the alcalde. Matagorda Bay was empty. The ship had sailed while they were talking to the padre.

"I've been so dad-blame stupid," Innis huffed.

Molly watched the color drain from his face, and she commented, "They were using the padre as a diversion, weren't they? At least we still have our weapons. And, we're still alive. They haven't tried to harm us."

"Not yet," Innis rejoined. "Give them time, and they will. They're probably afraid of us. You can bet they're watching us, and sizing us up right now. Maybe we can find another way out of here, another way back. Let's take this trail we're on and head west out of town. If we can get into the tall grass outside of town, we might be able to circle around and get back on the Gotier Trace. After that, I don't know. We'll figure it out when we get there, if we get there."

Half running and half walking, they followed the trail west and came immediately to the mouth of a swollen river. The water was high but calm at the shoreline where they stood. Brush and trees were submerged beyond them. Further out the river swelled and rippled, as a powerful current rushed swiftly into Matagorda Bay.

"Should we try to cross?" Molly asked. Kneeling and cupping her hands, she dipped the clear water and drank until she was full.

Innis waded in about knee deep, splashed his face, drank, and responded, "It don't look crossable, Molly. If our things get wet and my rifle won't fire, we'll be done for. And, that current out there looks like it would just sweep us out into the bay." He looked around. "Up there looks like marsh, and it looks flooded. We'll have to go back and make our way through town."

When they again entered town, they cut across the side streets, avoiding the Biladeau Cotton Works. Ducking between row houses, they jumped picket fences and plunged shoulder high into the grass north of town. Feeling safer, Molly pushed through the tall grass with Innis until they came out on the Gotier Trace.

Pausing to examine the road in both directions, it appeared deserted and safe. Once they were on the road, they made better time, and covered a great distance. After sunset they camped in a thicket, but did not build a fire, fearing that it could attract unwelcome attention.

By midmorning the next day they found their wagon. Molly climbed up, and said, "Looks like everything's still here, but now we don't have the means to haul anything."

Innis climbed up beside her. "Maybe we should have stayed here in the first place, Molly. Maybe we should have …" An expression of extreme pain swept over his face.

"Innis, what's wrong?"

He lifted his hand to his left arm, and Molly saw the point of an arrow projecting toward her through his sleeve below his shoulder. It had struck his arm from behind while they were talking.

"Innis! Have mercy! Innis!" she screamed.

In the direction of the arrow he swung his rifle around, shouldering and cocking the weapon, as another arrow thumped into his thigh. Groaning, he then shouted, "Get down! Get down!"

Over the backboard she leapt and crouched behind the sea-chest. Innis fired, and she could see a man thrown backwards, screaming, out in the brush, about ten or twelve paces from the wagon. He looked like one of the Comancheros they had seen the day before. Five others sprang up and charged at them from the brush, shooting at them with bow and arrow. An arrow thudded into the side of the sea-chest by Molly's head. Away from it she jumped, as another arrow landed in the back rest.

From his powder horn Innis pulled the stopper, as an arrow struck next to him, and then another. Into the barrel of his rifle he poured a charge of gun powder. Another arrow struck the sea-chest, and another the sideboard. Surrounding the wagon, the attackers set fresh arrows in their bows, pulled back and released them. An arrow thumped again into Innis, piercing his side. He grunted and rammed a ball down the barrel. A man stepped into the road in front of him and pulled a dueling pistol from his waist. Innis righted his rifle and pulled off the spent firing primer, then seated a fresh primer in its place, and cocked the trigger mechanism. The man on the road raised an old dueling pistol and fired. Molly heard the ball hit Innis through his chest with a sonorous thump, ripping out the back of his shirt. She couldn't believe what she was seeing. Innis fired. The man on the road went to his knees, and his pistol slipped from his fingers to the road. Climbing down from the wagon, Innis wielded his rifle by its barrel, and swung it at the kneeling man's head, like an axe splitting firewood.

Another man stepped out, and Molly recognized the evil-eyed Comanchero with the bushy hair and pointed beard. Raising his pistol, he shot Innis point blank.

From the grotesque sight Molly turned her eyes, unable to look anymore upon it. So sudden and unexpected was the attack that she didn't fully comprehend what had happened. From over her shoulder she drew her pitchfork and held it in front of her. Now she had to fight for her life. Leaping to her feet, she raised the pitchfork against her attackers. Jabbing at them, she tried to drive them back. One of them managed to snatch the pitchfork away from her. Then the evil-eyed Comanchero grabbed the hem of her dress and yanked her off the wagon to the ground, where he then held her.

Trapped and unable to move against his grasp, Molly's Irish blood began to boil and she flew into a rage. She kicked with every ounce of energy she could muster, but the bushy-haired Comanchero lifted her upside down by the hem of her dress, and encircled her thrashing legs with the pitchfork in his hand. Kicking with the heels of her rotten shoes, she battered his chest, face, and shoulders. A blow landing squarely on his nose stunned him. Dropping her hem and her, he stepped back and lifted his hand to the gushing froth of blood, which she had brought forth from his nostrils.

From his hands Molly jerked the pitchfork and turned it against him, lunging at him. Someone grabbed her from behind, as others tried to subdue her. Screaming and twisting from side to side, she wrenched an arm free and swung the pitchfork handle into a man's face. He stepped back, but the Comanchero who had grabbed her from behind had her yet. Tightening his grasp, he forced the air from her lungs. Tighter he squeezed.

Trying to catch her breath, she could not. Her ears began to ring, drowning out the sounds around her, and then blackness overwhelmed her.

BUFFALO HEAD

THIS COULDN'T BE happening. It had to be a dream. Standing on the loading dock at the Biladeau Cotton Works in Matagorda, she was bound and gagged. The laborers stood beside her and they were laughing at her. Behind her the alcalde called out to a crowd, which stood in front of the loading dock, "What am I bid for this lovely prize?"

"One hundred," someone bid.

"One fifty," bid another.

"Two hundred."

"Going once, going twice."

Her owners took her dress from her and put in its place a putrid rag. They beat her and bound her, and into a keelboat they threw her. Then they rowed her out to sea. Aboard a ship, they threw her into the ship's hold and chained her with other slaves. Regaining her senses she assessed her wretched surroundings, and with the other slaves she wallowed and slept in her own ordure. The horrid smell stopped her breath. Above her a grate of iron provided meager ventilation and above the grate the birds of the sea circled patiently, hungry for the flesh of those who would perish.

They brought food to her but she refused to eat, refused to be a slave, and prayed that starvation would set her free. Into her throat they slid a tube, forcing her to eat by pouring food into her stomach, and from there her spirit rose from her body. Above them she hovered and watched the palpations they laid upon her emaciated body.

With her the spirits of other slaves rose slowly through the planks forming the ship's deck. Passing through the deck upwards, she ascended above the shipmates and watched as they busily maintained the ship's apparatus. Upwards she continued through another deck and into the captain's quarters.

In a grand foyer she paused, and her feet rested upon a floor of cold, white marble. Massive pillars of granite surrounded her, rising to support an immense dome of green crystal and stone, a dome glowing with emerald light. Across the foyer a staircase of marble led to an upper deck. Made from the same marble as the floor, the stairway was lined with sculpted balusters, and capped by an emerald balustrade.

She expected the long climb to weary her but it was effortless. At the top she entered a broad passageway of speckled terrazzo floors and marble walls. Lining both sides of the passageway she found doorways, which opened into mysterious rooms, and the doors were all standing open. To the end of the hallway she could not see. Walking light-footed, she peered into each room she passed and thought she could see shadows, ominous figures, and armed oppressors inside. Hundreds of rooms she passed, checking inside each for danger before stepping in front of any open doorway. Finally, she could see the end of the passageway.

When she reached the end, she stood before arched double doors of solid ivory. Upon the doors was carved the images of men, fighting men, who pierced and struck each other, and men who wrestled in the throes of death, agonizing, and displaying their great pain. As she examined the images, the doors creaked slowly open.

Molly was frightened. Her hands shook, but she entered anyway. Inside she found an elaborate boudoir and an aristocrat. To her his back was turned, as if he'd been waiting for her. A long and silvery cloak covered his shoulders, and over the cloak a collar of white lace flowed. Around his neck was tied an ascot of purple silk, and from his head hung precisely trimmed ringlets of dark hair. Around him she detected a peculiar fragrance, a repulsive stench covered with lavender, a stench which reminded her of the ship's hold she'd risen from.

Glancing around the boudoir, she observed draperies of purple, which hung over rows of tall windows. Something like fur covered the floor, the thick fur of a bear, plush, and it too was purple. At the center of the boudoir stood a grand four poster, canopied with purple cloth, and surrounded by sheer white curtains. The bedcover was a cloud of purple and pillows floated above it.

The aristocrat turned to face her, and his fine clothes fell away. His hair went bushy and his eyes evil. She realized that he was the evil-eyed Comanchero. Before her he stood, and he was bare to his waistcloth and leggings. Grabbing her by her wrists, he pulled her next to him, and slithered his arms around her. She could feel the heat from his body, and could feel the butt of a dueling pistol behind his waistband. As he pressed his lips against hers, she wrapped her fingers around the pistol. Yanking it from his waistband, she thrust the barrel into his chest and pulled the trigger. Stepping back, she watched his lips part with surprise, and his eyes open with amazement. To the floor he slumped. Behind him the drapes fell from the windows. The walls fell away, and the boudoir dropped from under her feet. Stumbling, she realized that she was now standing on hardpan.

Alone in a prairie, a trail lay before her dividing the grasses, which smelled to her of sage. There was no water and no place to sleep. She was tired and so very thirsty. Her heart was pounding.

Believing that the trail would lead to a place of hope, she began to walk, and continued walking throughout the day until her legs throbbed. The prairie became thick with brush, standing higher than she was tall and it crowded her on both sides. When it closed together there was no trail left for her to follow.

On the ground she seated herself and rested. Reaching out, she discovered that the prairie grass was clogged with serried thorns and briars. As she withdrew her arm the thorns cut into her flesh. Lifting her arm to her lips, she could taste her own blood, and determined that she could walk the trail no further, except for a tunnel of sorts, which twisted through the brush away from her. At ground level she examined the tunnel, a wild animal trail, another way through the brush.

"Molly McCracken," someone whispered her name.

Every fiber in her body jolted. Then she replied, "I am here."

"Come this way."

On her hands and knees she crawled into the tunnel, pressing through the scratchy brush until her arms ached and her hands and knees burned. Throughout the evening she crawled as briars tore at her clothes and covered her body with stinging scratches. Pressing forward, she could see that her hands and knees left bloody tracks on the ground beneath her. Sunlight dwindled, but she kept going until she emerged in a grassy clearing.

The sun had set. Only starlight revealed the open space where she now stood. Her hands and knees burned. Standing before her she could see a large tree with black limbs twisting out and up into the heavens. In desperation she called out, "Where are you?"

"I am here."

Around the tree she stumbled and found standing on the other side a beautiful woman. Molly had seen the woman before in a dream; but this wasn't a dream, was it? The beautiful woman wore a white gown, and her hair was like black silk. Though the wind was not blowing, her gown and her hair flowed like water into the darkness behind her. Light emanated from within her and it grew in intensity as Molly beheld her. Against the bright light she shielded her eyes.

In the woman's arms she held a child wrapped in a brilliant white blanket, and in her hand she held a cup, like the one she'd held in her dream. The cup looked like a chalice cast in fine gold. Molly could almost touch it, and on it she could see carvings, like men riding horses. Their eyes were bright rubies, and in their hands they held diamonds like bolts of lightning.

"Take this cup," the woman placed the chalice in Molly's hands. "Now turn the cup around. What do you see?"

The cup was filled with deep red liquid and it felt heavy in Molly's hands. She turned it and found the image of a single mounted warrior with flowing hair, jeweled eyes, and lightning in both hands.

"Now drink," the woman instructed her.

"What is this?" Molly asked.

The woman explained, "It is the cup of the fury of the wrath of the Almighty. You and this cup will be as one. Now you understand in part, but soon you will understand all things."

"I can't do this," Molly said, and returned the cup to the beautiful woman.

Holding out the child, the woman said, "Take this child."

Molly lifted the corner of the blanket from the youngster's face, and saw Amy smiling up at her and saying, "Lub you, Aunt Lolly."

"Oh, my!" Molly gasped and fell backwards, away from the woman, and landing on her back in the grass. From there a strange force drew her backwards from the clearing into the thicket. The beautiful woman shrank from her view as she yelled, "Amy!"

The briars closed around her, and darkness enveloped her. On the grassy plain her withdrawal increased in speed until she re-emerged into the boudoir. The evil-eyed Comanchero lay yet in a pool of blood and his blood seeped between the floorboards. Covering her mouth, she cried, "This is impossible," and angrily swiped tears from her cheeks.

Up the hallway the strange force dragged her backwards, past the shadowy rooms to the grand foyer, and onto the ship's deck she was thrown. Reaching out to catch herself, her hands passed through the ship's apparatus, through the shipmates, and through the deck planks. Landing on her hands and knees, she lifted her gaze and found herself on the loading dock at the Biladeau Cotton Works. The laborers were laughing at her. The alcalde laughed at her as she stood up and then fainted.

Oh, my! Oh, my! Molly screamed, as she suddenly awakened, and just as suddenly realized that her screams were only in her mind. The ship, the boudoir, the thicket, and the beautiful woman were a frightening nightmare. Fully awake, she noticed that she was lying under the seat-board of a wagon, and she was tied hand and foot.

The wagon was moving, jittering over a rough road, and she could tell that it was a large wagon, not her wagon. Recalling the attack which killed Innis, she began to weep for him, and her tears dampened the floorboards where she lay. The day passed and her tears flowed. Then, numb with grief, she writhed out from under the seat-board and sat up to see where she was.

The Comanchero with the disfigured and tattooed face drove the wagon. Glancing down, he shook his head at her, as if warning her not to get up and nodded toward a mounted Comanchero who rode ahead of the wagon. She recognized the evil-eyed Comanchero with the bushy hair and pointed beard.

"You see my friend up there with big nose, like lemon?" the disfigured Comanchero asked her. "His hair it is bushy and his beard it is pointed like Buffalo. He is called Buffalo Head. I think he will keel you."

Sinking back to the floorboards, Molly began again to weep. Sensing that the wagon was on the Gotier Trace, she had noticed that the sun was setting on her left. That meant they were traveling north toward Missis Powell's Tavern. The wagon had been filled with wooden crates and barrels and those were lashed together with rope. She believed that she was in the same freight wagon she'd seen at the Biladeau Cotton Works in Matagorda. Ahead, she'd seen mounted men, five of them with the evil-eyed Comanchero named Buffalo Head. Alongside the wagon, she'd seen others walking, and behind them more Comanchero's followed on foot.

Slowly pulling the reins through his fingers, the disfigured Comanchero watched her, and said, "I would not like you mad at me, señora. You keek like mule. Buffalo Head, he would cut my throat, if I break his nose, like you break his nose. You shame him bad, señora. We laugh at him, and call him Big Nose, because it was woman who break his nose. We laugh long time. Now he get plenty mad. Maybe he cut you. Maybe he keel you. Maybe he just keep you for himself."

As the sun began to set, Molly sat up again. Buffalo Head guided the wagons into a clear place beside a large tree with black limbs, which twisted out and up into the darkening sky. Dismounting, as his men unhitched the wagon and strung the horses together by a creek, Buffalo Head pulled a double-edged dagger from a scabbard at his side. Clenching the thin ivory handle in his fist, he turned his attention to Molly and rushed to her. Grabbing her arm, he thrust his dagger.

Exhausted, helpless, and tightly bound, she leaned away from him. There was nothing she could do to resist or avoid him, nothing she could do but prepare to receive his revenge. Closing her eyes, she clenched her teeth and whispered, "Please, help me."

"Que?" Buffalo Head asked as he thrust his dagger beneath the bindings that held her hands, cutting them and then pulling her down from the wagon to the ground.

Lame and stiff, she slumped onto her knees, but he yanked her again to her feet and pressed his face against hers. She could smell his sour breath. It turned her stomach and she looked away.

"Look at me, señora," he growled, "so you can see what you have done to me."

She would not look at him.

Violently he shook her and she felt the vertebrae in her back popping as he yelled, "Look at me!"

"Oh, my!" she gasped, and cringed with the pain he caused in her arm and in her back. Turning her face to him, nose to nose, she looked into the bottomless black pits that were his evil, coal black eyes. In their depths she perceived his hatred and understood that she was about to die.

Buffalo Head pressed the flat of his blade against the side of his swollen nose and said, "You will pay for this, señora. You will pay plenty mucho. Or maybe, I will sell you to the dogs of the sea. Or maybe, I will keel you now." He cranked his head toward the disfigured Comanchero and yelled, "Why are you laughing at me, stupido?"

The disfigured Comanchero's amusement faded instantly.

"Make fire," Buffalo Head shouted at him. "I am hungry, and I am thirsty." Then he shoved Molly toward him and the disfigured Comanchero caught her as she stumbled to the ground. "Put my bedroll and saddle over there and tie her to that tree. Watch her until I return." Into the darkness Buffalo head sauntered.

The disfigured Comanchero dragged her by her arms over to a giant live oak. Seating her against the trunk, he bound her hands in front of her, and tied the rope around the tree, cinching her to it. Casting her gaze along the black limbs twisting out and up into the heavens, she tried to move but couldn't. Quietly, she watched as the other Comancheros made camp.

While they knocked down brush and built a fire, one of them carried into camp a bundle under his arm. It was a blanket, neatly wrapped to protect something. Kneeling, he opened the bundle, and up popped a blonde head. A little girl rubbed her eyes, and looked around.

"Amy!" Molly screamed, and her heart raced. "Amy! You're still alive! It's me! It's me!"

"Aunt Lolly," the toddler cried.

The Comanchero stood the little girl on her feet and nudged her toward Molly. She ran to her, spreading her little arms, and pumping her little legs beneath her ankle length dress.

Molly wanted to scoop her up, and she struggled against her bindings, heaving her elbows from side to side. Amy jumped onto her lap and threw her arms around Molly's neck, as joyful tears streamed down Molly's cheeks. Nothing seemed to matter now that Amy was here. The warmth of her little body gave Molly hope, something she had not known since she left Gonzales.

"Where's mommy?" Amy asked.

Molly swallowed but couldn't answer. For Amy's sake she fought back her grief and choked out her words, "She's coming. You'll see."

"When is she coming, Aunt Lolly?"

"Soon, sweetie. She'll be here soon."

Around the campfire the Comancheros sat cross-legged. Flames illuminated their smudged faces as they passed around a bottle and ate dried meat, which they called tasso. Some divided a large cake of bread, which one had brought in a grain sack.

Buffalo Head joined them, opened another bottle, and filled his cup from it. Taking bread and meat out of the hand of the man next to him, he ate of it and said, "I tell you this will not be easy, but you do not listen. I tell you wait. I tell you we will take them without fight, but you do not listen to me. Vacas estúpidas! Now Two-Feathers and Robolo, they do not ride with us no more because you are stupid cows and do not wait like I say wait." He flung the contents of his mug at them, splattering three of the Comancheros, who sat across the campfire from him. Standing, he pulled his dagger and pointed it at them. "I think maybe it is you that should ride no more, sí?"

Three Comancheros jumped and stumbled backwards, away from the fire, leaving their supper, to which the others then helped themselves. Buffalo Head sheathed his knife and reseated himself, shouting, "Bring me the rifle."

A Comanchero brought to Buffalo Head the rifle, which had belonged to Innis. Molly recognized it. This seemed to please him, for he examined the full length of it and turned it over in his hands. "This bring maybe twenty dollar," he said. "But, I keep this. We need many more rifles, and we need horses." He pointed at Amy. "This one, maybe we trade." Lifting his gaze to Molly, he said, "This one, she bring two hundred dollar, maybe three hundred. Maybe I keep her. Or maybe I keel her now and make me very much happy."

His threat caused a flutter of fear in Molly's heart as Amy clung to her neck and nestled her face against her shoulder.

Tossing his head toward the three offenders, Buffalo Head continued, "You get nothing. Maybe we get hundred pesos for supplies we take to army, so," he waved at those sitting around the fire, "all of you get five pesos each except these three. Maybe next time you wait when I say wait. Maybe, next time we do better."

One of the Comancheros sprang to his feet followed by another who was pulling his knife. Molly thought they were attacking Buffalo Head. Then she heard something in the thicket and Buffalo Head sprang to his feet. Out of the thicket and into the light of the campfire stepped a native.

Both sides of the native's hair were braided and intertwined with brightly colored feathers. His arms were bare and his breast piece was sewn into angular ribs of bright red and yellow. Tousled animal skin covered his legs and in his hand he wielded a blade, not a blade of stone as natives normally carried, but a blade of steel. Molly wasn't sure if he was Comanche or Kiowa, most likely Kiowa because he was tall and heavily built. He made a gesture that indicated a greeting.

Buffalo Head returned the gesture and motioned that the Kiowa should join him at the fire. They seemed to know each other and sat down together. The Comancheros tucked their knives at their waists, returned to the fire, and finished their meals. The Kiowa signaled for others to join him. Then three more emerged from the shadows, and sat with him by the fire.

The disfigured Comanchero brought to Molly a crust of bread, several strips of tasso and a cup. Untying her hands, he stood by, gesturing that she should feed Amy. The toddler ate hungrily, as if she hadn't eaten for more than a day, and then she fell asleep on Molly's shoulder. Molly was thirsty and lifted the cup Amy drank from and she was thankful to have a little water.

The Kiowa man rose with Buffalo Head from the campfire, approached Molly and into his arms he took Amy. The disfigured Comanchero tied Molly again to the tree. As the Kiowa man took Amy away, Molly screamed at him, "Where are you going! You can't take her! Bring her back to me! You can't have her! Bring her back, please!"

He did not answer her, and walked into the darkness the way he'd come. Buffalo Head followed him and moments later she could hear horses clopping away.

Buffalo Head returned and he was smiling. "Two good horses," he informed the others. "They trade two good horses for girl with yellow hair. This one," he indicated Molly, "I keep." Approaching the live oak where she was tied, he spread his feet about shoulder width, and stood close enough for her to feel the heat from his body. "And now," he said. "It is time for you." Turning his head, he paused and listened, as if hearing something. "Horses," he said to the others and gestured to his men that they should go to the road and see who was approaching.

Scrambling to their feet, the Comancheros fanned out into the dark thicket. Taking up the rifle, which had belonged to Innis, Buffalo Head went with them.

Molly could hear them out on the road, speaking together in Spanish. When they had finished, Buffalo Head returned to the campfire. With him she recognized the laborers from the loading dock in Matagorda. "You, you, and you." Buffalo Head directed his men. "Come with me." He pointed to the disfigured Comanchero, and instructed him, "You are in charge until I return. Take the wagon to General Urrea and wait for me there." He glared at Molly. "This one you will save for me. You will let nothing happen to her."

With three of his men and the laborers from the dock, he left. She watched them walk into the darkness and heard their horses clop away. Unrolling their bedrolls without taking their eyes from her, the remaining Comancheros constantly gawked at her. The disfigured Comanchero appointed those who would keep watch through the night and then he untied

Molly. With the rope, which had held her to the tree, he tied her hand and foot and tethered her to his own waist. Then he provided her with a blanket, and indicated that she should lay on it, as he laid himself upon his own bedroll.

Heavy with her burden of grief she lay upon her back, gazing up through the twisting branches into the heavens. Everything in the world had been taken from her. Hopeless tears ran over her cheeks and into her ears. She longed for Amy, mourned for Innis, and missed her beloved sister, Emily; but she refused to reveal any of her feelings to the disfigured Comanchero. Fighting back her tears, she bit her lip and let not a single sob or a whimper escape from her.

Images of her loved ones swam through her thoughts. She couldn't stop them. Over and over she relived the shootings and the horrors. Waves of sorrow washed over her until her eyes had swollen and the stars above her merged into a sparkly blur. She could yet see the alcalde laughing at her. His deception killed Innis and put Amy in the hands of the Kiowa. His trickery put her in the hands of the evil-eyed Buffalo Head.

Turning on her side, she inadvertently tugged on the tether connecting her to the disfigured Comanchero. Holding her breath, she expected him to rise against her, but he did not wake up.

Looking around she examined the tree she'd been tied to, and expected to see the beautiful woman in white standing behind it. Only grass stood behind the tree, starlight and grass. Her heart was slowing and her breath deepening. Beads of sweat trickled from her face into her hair and her stomach was sour. When she had relaxed enough to collect her thoughts, she felt around for the knots in the rope that held her. Never had she encountered a knot that she could not untie and these her nimble fingers untied easily.

Glancing around, she considered making a run for it and peered into the darkness where she knew Gotier Trace would be. The Comancheros would look for her there, even if she didn't go that way. She knew the river was close by, somewhere beyond the thicket. She could smell water. Twisting around again to look at the live oak behind her, she also noticed a thicket beyond the tree, and at ground level she could see an opening. It looked like a tunnel made by an animal but too small for a man. It was not an inviting place to go, for she knew it was filled with thorns and briars, but she could fit through that opening. Of course, she thought, that made it perfect. They would never find her in there. They wouldn't be able to follow her and they wouldn't expect her to escape that way.

She looked again at the silhouette of the disfigured Comanchero sleeping next to her and then over at the one whom he'd appointed to watch the camp that night. The night watchman had propped up his knees and he'd folded his arms over them. His head drifted down to his arms and he did not lift it up again. She could see his chest heave deep and slow and she waited. Whatever they had been drinking had taken them thankfully into a deep slumber.

The fire dwindled to glowing coals and she guessed that an hour or more had passed. She tried to crawl away, but her dress caught beneath her knees. Pulling it up to her waist, she tied it together. Pausing to listen, she could hear only the snoring sounds of deep sleep.

Crawling a short distance, she paused again. There was no other sound except snoring. Twenty more paces and she was beyond the tree and at the edge of the thicket. On her stomach she dragged herself into the opening. Once inside, she waited until her eyes adjusted to the darkness. When the ground came into focus, she looked ahead and saw a labyrinth of tunnels turning through the thicket in every direction. As she wormed her way into the largest, something grabbed her hair, and her heart skipped a beat.

Fumbling with the briars above her head, she tried to make as little noise as possible, and discovered that a branch of thorns had pulled her bonnet off and snagged her hair. Of all the dumb, unlucky things to happen, she thought. Against the ground she pressed her face and used both hands to free herself. Again she pushed ahead. As she did, thorns caught on her back, and tore her flesh.

The tunnel broadened, and she was able to get up on her hands and knees. Moving faster, she came out in a clear space and stood. Looking around in the starlight, she noticed that she was surrounded by thicket on all sides. Walking was easier than crawling, so she walked quickly and in doing so walked straight into a patch of prickly pear. The spines imbedded in her thighs. Backing away, she pulled out the painful spines one by one and heard someone yelling.

"Ella escapó!"

Very close to her she heard a great commotion and she realized that the tunnel she'd crawled through had taken her in a circle. She was still at the Comanchero's encampment.

THE THICKET

HOLDING PERFECTLY STILL, Molly listened as the Comancheros searched the brush around her. She hoped they could not see her. Crashing through the thicket, their search moved farther away, as they kicked the brush and yelled at each other.

Searching for something that would lead her away from them, she looked up into the sky. Choosing the brightest star in a direction opposite from the camp, she decided to follow it. Unsure what direction it was, she was sure that it would lead her away, rather than taking her in circles.

A few cautious steps and she walked into another patch of prickly pear. Something ran out from under her feet, a critter. She wanted to scream, but covered her mouth and jumped back. As she did, she jumped into another patch of prickly pear. Lifting one arm, and then the other, she removed spines from the backs of her arms, and tried to remove the spines imbedded across the middle of her back but couldn't reach them. Next time she wouldn't be so jumpy.

At the edge of the clearing she encountered briars and dropped to her hands and knees. Crawling, and then standing when she could, she checked the location of that bright star. Pushing herself to her limit, she put as much distance as possible between her and the Comancheros. Crawling until her hands and knees burned, she could yet hear the Comancheros calling to each other and crashing through the thicket behind her.

The tunnel she followed turned sharply and ended at a massive obstruction. Reaching out, she determined that a tree had fallen over the tunnel. Broken branches protruded in every direction from the trunk. Reaching again, she touched the trunk, and her hand broke through. The trunk was rotten. Withdrawing her hand, she also withdrew with it a salamander, which promptly ran up her arm and into her hair. This made her earnestly want to scream, but she clamped her lips together. Shaking her hair with the fingers of both her hands, she made the creature fall out and scamper away.

The windfall was overgrown with briars. She could not see past it or from one end to the other. Crawling over it would make too much noise, so she worked her way down to the base of the tree. There she found a small animal tunnel and crawled through. The tunnel turned and she followed it up the other side of the windfall, and searched for a way out of the briars. Putting her hand down, she heard a loud hiss, an unmistakable sound. Screaming, she backed away from it. Bolting up, she crashed through the dry branches above her head.

It was too dark to see if what she'd heard was a rattle snake, but she didn't want to take that kind of chance. She had heard that hissing sound before on the farm, but there was always someone around to dispatch an unwanted rattler. Innis would stomp on them with his high-top boots. Emmet would crush their heads with the end of a stick. Never had she dealt with a rattler herself and never had she been so dangerously close to one. Looking down through the dry branches at her feet, she could see by the light of the stars a possum. Its mouth was open, and its teeth were bare. It hissed at her again, and with her foot she shooed it away.

"Ella está aquí!" she heard someone yell.

One of the Comancheros must have heard her scream, and she guessed that he was about a hundred paces away. Very quiet, she stood and listened, as he crunched through the brush toward her. Turning, she tried to run, but couldn't push her way through the razor sharp briars. To her hands and knees she dropped again, and crawled as fast as she could.

Whenever the brush thinned, she pumped her hands and knees faster to get away. When she could, she would stand and run, until encountering another windfall. She encountered millions of them, all different kinds, and all covered with briars, which always forced her down onto her hands and knees to find a way around them. A critter ran up the tunnel ahead of her, and she realized that they didn't frighten her anymore.

When she was able to stand, she checked the location of the star, adjusted her direction, and noticed a glow over the thicket. The glow would be the sunrise coming up in the east, and that meant she had been going north. Again, thick brush forced her to crawl. This time she felt soft grass under her hands, and then she also felt it under her knees. Into a small, kidney shaped, grassy clearing she entered and rolled onto her back. Gazing up into the morning sky, she listened, to be certain that no one else was nearby.

Mosquitoes would not let her rest, and they swarmed on her exposed skin in the open. Swatting at them, she realized how sore her hands were, and sat up to examine them. Her knees and her hands were bloody and swollen and her pantalets hung from her thighs in shreds. When she looked back the way she'd come, she could see tracks of blood, which her hands and knees had left in the grass. Recalling her dream, she pondered the portent of the bloody tracks and the prescience of the woman in white, and wondered if the tunnels would take her to Amy.

As quietly as she could, she untied her dress from her waist, and tore it into strips to use as bandages. After wrapping her knees and hands, she looked around. A live oak stood on the far side of the clearing. Climbing it, she searched in every direction, and found that the thicket surrounded her as far as she could see. The river had to be close but was nowhere in sight. Her heart raced, for she realized that she had escaped from the Comancheros, but had also become hopelessly lost.

Emmet told her once that thickets along creeks and swampy areas could be several miles wide and she feared that she was lost in one of those places. If she had gone east, she would have come out on Gotier Trace and probably would have been recaptured. If west, she would have come out at the river, but she suspected that the Comancheros would look for her there, too. She decided to stay in the thicket where she felt safe.

Pulling back her hair, she knotted it to make it shorter and keep it from catching in the thorns. With a strip of cloth she tied it to keep it from coming apart. She learned to manipulate the thorns in the animal tunnels with a stick that she'd picked up along the way. Soon, she was slipping through the tunnels almost as fast as the critters that ran out ahead of her, and she couldn't hear the Comancheros anymore.

Birds sang morning songs in the brush above her, and when she came to another windfall, she seated herself upon it and rested. The bandages on her hands were already worn and bloody and her knees were wearing through. She tore new strips from her dress and added them to her worn bandages.

The soil under her feet seemed damper than before and the air smelled musty. She thought she could hear water and down to the ground she crouched for a better look. Into the thicket she crawled until she found a creek about a foot wide. It wasn't the river, but it was water, and she was thirsty. Briars kept her from reaching the water. Laying flat and squeezing into a tunnel, she pulled herself toward the creek, until her hands sank into the ground. Unexpectedly, she sank up to her elbows. "This is no good," she said, and wiggled backwards until she was out of the mud.

Exhausted, she rolled over on a bed of damp moss and gazed up through the interlocking briars above her. A bird landed overhead, chirping and fluttering. If only she were that bird, she could fly away from her thorn briar prison. Recalling her dream, the briars overhead reminded her of the iron grate over the ship's hold. Recalling the flesh eating birds above the grate, she shuddered. Closing her eyes, she imagined that she was that little bird flying away.

When she woke up, she discovered that the thicket had become hot, uncomfortably hot. The air wasn't moving, and her thirst was greater than ever. The little, muddy creek she'd found should flow to the river, she reasoned. If she could find a way to follow the creek, it would lead her to the river. The risk of being seen by the Comancheros was worth a drink of cool water. Crawling away from the creek, she found a tunnel, twisting, winding, but generally parallel to the creek. Listening, she could hear a trickle from the creek, and then crawled into the tortuous tunnel, hoping it would take her to the river. Like all the others, she forced her way through, crawling around windfalls, and listening for the reassuring trickle of the creek beside her.

The intense afternoon heat clouded her thoughts. Becoming dizzy, she noticed that she had stopped perspiring. Needing water soon, she teetered forward until her hands again sank into the ground. Placing her stick in her teeth, she crawled ahead and sank deeper. As she struggled through the mud, she noticed that the tunnel had broadened. Pushing forward, she could see water filling the tunnel ahead. If she had to, she would swim through the mud to reach the river.

Then up to her elbows she sank. Below the mud she felt solid ground, breathed a sigh of relief, and crawled into the water. The cool water and mud restored her senses, but she jolted when a black snake squirmed past her.

Any other time a snake in the water would have sent her into a screaming panic, but instead she pushed it away with her stick. She was convinced that the river was not far away.

In the open she crawled from the thicket into the river and sat in the shallows beside the riverbank, alert to the possible presence of alligators. The water was slow and the current gently soothed her overheated and injured body. She dunked her head, and then cupped her hands to drink. Catching her breath, she drank again, long and deep.

The thicket along the riverbank was covered with spring blossoms, mostly white, but also dotted with yellow and sprinkled with red, which added some joy to her briefly refreshing moment. The river was swollen and broad. Out at the center she could see the current bulging up in a rush of ripples. Standing, wobbly and stiff, she walked knee-deep against the current along the bank, pulled up and munched the shoots of spring wapato. Walking in the water was slow and tiresome, but the bottom was gravely, and she didn't think her hands and knees could take any more crawling.

Further up, the banks spread into a broad marsh. Through it the river deepened. Chest deep she waded, keeping a watchful eye out for alligators, until the banks again rose into a thicket. When it did, the ground seemed to rise higher than before, and there were more trees, bigger trees. Heading ashore for a closer look, she decided she would find a suitable tree and climb it to assess whatever was up ahead.

Perched upon the outward twisting limb of a live oak, she observed that the thicket transitioned into a grassy plain a mile or so beyond the riverbank. She could hardly believe her eyes when she noticed five riders moving south along the edge of the thicket, leaving behind them a cloud of dust, which drifted into the sky. Gotier Trace must run along the edge of the thicket, she thought, and the riders could be Comancheros, and they could be searching for her. Fearing not that she would be seen from her vantage point in the live oak, she noted that the distance was great, the thicket vast, and the branches and leaves where she stood gave her adequate cover.

Behind her the sun was settling. On her left she spotted a patch of green at the edge of the grassy plain. It was, maybe, a pasture a couple miles up. Determined to reach the pasture before dark, she climbed down, walked when she could, and crawled again through the briars when she couldn't walk.

Darkness had fallen over the thicket before she reached the pasture. Up to a split-rail fence she crawled, and the fence was evidence to her that she'd finally reached civilization. Standing, wobbling, and hoping to find a homestead, she climbed over the fence and stepped out into the pasture. Twilight lingered yet in the open, illuminating large, white stones that were strewn over the pasture. As she approached them her knees buckled and she became faint, but her heart leapt as she realized that what she thought were stones were actually cows. She yelled, "Cows, beautiful, beautiful cows!"

Attempting to run to them, she stumbled and fell. Picking herself up, she staggered to the nearest cow and clung to its fur. Coaxing it, she said, "It's time to go home now. Show me where your home is." With great surprise, she released the animal, for it smelled bad. The cow was dead and had apparently been dead for quite some time. To the next one she staggered. It too was dead. She was dizzy, and lifted her hand to her forehead to steady herself. Glancing around, she realized that the pasture was filled with dead cows, and then her eyes caught movement across the pasture. It was a man, and he was running. The man was running straight at her.

Comanchero!

A wave of panic drove the dizziness from her head. She'd forgotten about the Comancheros, forgot that they could see her out in the open. Turning toward the fence, she tried to run but her feet would not cooperate, and she fell onto her hands. It was useless, she'd been found and now she was captured.

"You're a woman!" a voice rumbled above her. She felt a hand on her shoulder. "Let me help you, ma'am."

"You're not a Comanchero?" she asked.

"No, ma'am. I was too tall and too good looking. They only wanted short, ugly folks. And, I wasn't stupid enough either." Up onto her hands she pushed herself, as he hooked her arm and lifted. "Looks like you've been ruffled up."

To stop the pasture from spinning she again lifted her hand to her forehead and said, "I thought you were a Comanchero. I thought I had been captured again."

"I'm not a Comanchero, ma'am. I am Captain Williams of the Texas Rangers, San Antonio. I've been dispatched here by General Sam Houston."

"I remember you." She recognized his long, sandy, wavy hair and ghost-blue eyes. She recalled that he stood out because he was clean shaven, but now he had a growth of sandy colored whiskers covering his face. "You were riding with Houston when we were running from Gonzales," she said.

"Yes, ma'am."

"I asked one of your men to call you over, so I could ask you about my husband, Emmet."

"I don't recall that, ma'am. Sorry."

"I didn't see you again after that." She proceeded to detail everything that had happened to her, Amy, Emily, and Innis since they left Gonzales, adding, "So, last night, I escaped from the Comancheros by crawling into the thicket."

"You've been in the thicket since last night?" he asked.

"Yes." Her knees began to buckle again.

Catching her arm, he steadied her. "Would y'all like me to take you up to the cabin? The folks that were living there left a lot of things behind, clothes and such."

"Food?" she asked, and this time her knees did buckle, refusing to hold her up any longer. She slumped from his grasp.

Lifting her, he cradled her in his arms and said, "Hope y'all don't mind if I carry you, ma'am. You don't look like you're walking very well."

"I'm dizzy."

"Don't fret, ma'am. I got you now. Mercy, you're nothing but bones. What'd them Comancheros do to you anyway?"

"I've been sick, Mister Williams."

"Well, first thing, let's get you up to the cabin. I've got plenty of food up there, and stuff for making bandages. Your clothes are all shredded and bloody. There's lots of fresh clothes up there."

"Obliged, Mister Williams."

"That's why I'm here, ma'am."

Across the pasture he took a path to a dark cabin. Inside, he laid her on a rope-bed. The mattress was stuffed with straw, she could smell it, and it was covered with a blanket. In the bed she sank almost to the earthen floor. He removed his hat and struck a Vesuvian with his thumbnail. Flaring up, the flash revealed log walls, shuttered windows on opposite sides, and a log structure above, which supported a low, slanted roof. At the center of the floor a table had a tallow candle and candleholder upon it. He held the flame to the candle, and the flame climbed up onto the wick, brightening the cabin's interior. Before the Vesuvian went out, he took it over to a stick-and-mud chimney with an open hearth, and lit a handful of kindling.

"I'll put some water on the fire for you," he said. "There's jerked beef in that bag over there. Help yourself when you're up to it. We jerked enough to last a month or so. We had to exflunctícate the rest of the cattle before Santa Anna gets his hands on them." Captain Williams ducked his head, as he went out through the doorway saying, "There's clothes next to the chamber pot at the end of that bed you're lying on."

"Where are you going?" she asked.

"I'm going to wait outside while you get yourself cleaned up and dressed."

When the door had closed, she tried to pull her dress over her head, and found that it had stuck to her arms and to her back. Soaking a rag and wetting the fabric released the dried blood, but the prickly pear spines were imbedded yet in her back. "Ugh," she groaned, as she pulled her dress free from them. Holding up the tatters that had been her dress, she considered what a mess the thicket had made of it and of her. Into the corner she tossed the tattered dress. Washing her scratches gave her some relief and she finally pushed those rotten shoes off her feet.

She found clothing that she could tear into bandages, and then wrapped the bandages around her arms from her shoulders to her hands, and from her thighs down to her ankles. Then she pulled on a pair of trousers. The folks who had lived there hadn't left behind any dresses and the trousers were too big. The excess fabric she had to tie into a knot at her waist. Rinsing and shaking out her hair, she tied it back with a strip of bandage cloth and then took a seat on one of the chairs. Covering herself with a shirt from the clothes pile, she raised her voice and called out, "Mister Williams, would y'all mind coming in here please?"

Through the doorway he ducked inside. When he noticed her bare back, he diverted his eyes from her, and said, "Ma'am, you're not fully dressed. I can't …"

"It's alright, Mister Williams. I'd be obliged if y'all would be so kind as to remove the thorns from my back. I cannot reach them myself."

"Have mercy," he exclaimed as he pulled a chair up behind her. "They're imbedded, ma'am. Can you turn to the light a little more? Mercy, mercy, this is going to hurt you."

"Please do whatever you have to, Mister Williams."

He drew a Bowie from a sheath on his belt, a large Bowie, and with the tip of it he pried up a thorn. Then clamping the end of the thorn between the edge of the blade and his thumb, he pulled it out.

"Oh, that burns," Molly exclaimed.

"Sorry, ma'am."

"Molly. My name is Molly McCracken."

"Missis?" he asked.

"Yes, I'm Missis McCracken," she replied, and explained to him how Emmet had gone missing.

"Sorry to hear that, Missis McCracken. Sorry to hear about all of it. You seem like such a nice person, but I'm afraid a lot of good folks, like your husband, have been lost in the war."

"Lost yes, he's lost, but I fear now that he might also be dead."

He pulled another thorn from her back, and said, "These will get infected, if we don't get all of them out. The last thing you need is infection with everything else that's happened to you."

"I know. I know. Please continue, Captain Williams."

"The boys call me Boots," he explained, as he pried up another thorn.

"Ouch! That's an unusual name, Mister Boots."

Kicking his foot out, he rested his heel next to her chair, where she could see it. From heel to toe his boot was not much shorter than the seat of her chair, and was by far the largest boot she'd ever seen.

Observing the size of his feet, she understood how he'd acquired his nickname, and she announced, "I understand, Mister Boots."

Withdrawing his foot, he informed her, "Did you know your ribs are sticking out, Missis McCracken. Why don't you eat some of that jerked beef over there when were finished? Looks like you need it. I'm just about done. Then I'll go back outside. I don't have anything else to give you, except coffee."

Standing, he abruptly bumped his head on a roof beam. "Ouch," he mumbled. Stooping over, he reset his hat saying, "Short folks must've built this place." Leaving the cabin, he closed the door behind him. "Bar the door," he said from outside. "I'll sleep in the shed tonight."

Finding a large, floppy red shirt, she pulled it on over her bandages, and climbed onto the rope bed. Safe, dry, sheltered from mosquitoes, and totally exhausted, she fell instantly asleep.

The next morning she dragged herself, lame, burning, and sore, out of bed, and opened the shutters. She was savoring a strip of jerked beef when a knock came from the cabin door.

Boots had a coffee pot, freshly brewed, in one hand. In the other he held a grain sack, about a quarter full, and said, "Found this in the shed this morning. Haven't looked around in there much before this." He held the sack out to her and she took it.

Though the sack was almost empty, she found it too heavy to hold in her weakened condition, so she set it on the table and said, "Obliged, Mister Boots."

"It's oats," he explained. "The folks that lived here probably kept them for their horses. Found some rodents out there too. I think they wanted them oats as bad as I did. I had to arm wrestle them for it. There's still enough for us to make something though, bread if y'all feel up to it."

Excited by the prospect of having bread to eat, Molly didn't know if she had the energy to make it. "I might need help," she said.

"I'll help you," he offered and seated himself at the table. "I figured I could grind it if y'all want to make it into bread."

On a shelf next to the chimney she'd noticed a mortar and pestle the night before. Taking it down, she remarked, "These folks must have left in a hurry to leave this behind." Setting the mortar and pestle before Boots, she added, "I found a crock of bear oil, too. I can make flat bread." From the shelf she took down two tin cups, poured coffee and pulled up a chair.

"You look pale this morning," he observed. "Are you feeling all right?"

"Everything hurts, Mister Boots. I can hardly move my arms or my legs."

"My coffee will wake the dead, Missis McCracken." From his cup he took a sip, and added, "The boys like it that way. It might even get your arms and legs moving again."

Taking her first sip, she swallowed hard and said, "Yes, I see what you mean, Mister Boots."

While grinding a handful of oats into flour he said, "Now, let me tell you about the boys. They'll be back in a couple days. They're escorting some folks from Matagorda over to Harrisburg. We're finding that marauders are trying to move in on us, like the ones that ambushed you and your brother-in-law. They prey on unsuspecting folks. They've been raiding farms and pillaging and looting them. General Houston sent us down here to protect folks from incursions and depredations while they're fleeing from Santa Anna. We're using this farm as a temporary station."

She gazed over the rim of her cup at his narrow nose, and watched the sculpture of his lips, as they moved with his words. He was every bit as handsome as he was a gentleman, she thought.

"Missis McCracken?" he asked. "Are you getting all this? I said we'll go after the Comancheros when the boys get back."

"Yes, of course. Much obliged."

"Are you sure you're feeling all right?"

"Yes, I'm all right. I'm better now that I've had your coffee, I think."

"I was saying that I'm the only one here right now, and it's going to take me and all my boys if we want to catch those Comancheros that ambushed you. There's too many of them for me to go after them by myself."

"Yes, I heard that part. Please continue, Mister Boots."

"I heard wagons out on Gotier Trace last night. So, I went out for a look-see. By the time I got out to the road they were gone. Folks don't normally travel at night. I think it was the Comancheros you told me about. From what you've said, I'd say they're smuggling supplies up to Santa Anna. When the boys get back, we'll go after them. For now you're safe.

"If you don't mind staying here by yourself today, I'll go on down and find the place where you were ambushed and have a look around. Then I'll try to find the camp you escaped from. Maybe I can figure out where they took your niece."

"I don't mind staying here by myself, Mister Boots. I don't mind at all if it helps you find Amy."

He opened his jacket and she could see the butts of two pistols behind his belt. One of them he pulled, and laid it on the table before her.

"Guns scare me, Mister Boots."

"You ever shot one before?"

"My husband, Emmet, tried to teach me to shoot his rifle one time. It was too big and heavy. I had trouble holding it up. He had to help me hold it. Then when I fired it, it knocked me to the ground. I had a bruise on my shoulder for two weeks. He thought it was funny. Said he hoped I'd never have to defend myself."

"That's an unfortunate story, Missis McCracken. I'd never put my rifle in the hands of a lady like you. And, if I did, I wouldn't start you off with a full charge of powder. Here," He picked up the pistol. "Let me explain how this works. The charge is a lot smaller than what you put in a rifle. It's made to be fired from your hand, and not from your shoulder."

"That is a strange looking pistol." she noted.

"It's a repeater. They call it a Paterson. There's been other repeaters around, but not like this one. It's one of a kind. I went to Paterson, New Jersey, to get the first run and try them out myself." He pointed the weapon across the cabin and cocked the hammer. "They made it special for us Rangers. See here, the cylinder rotates when you cock it and brings up a fresh load, and cocking it also brings down the trigger out of the frame. When it's in the safe position, the trigger stays up inside so it won't catch on your clothing. Other than that, you pull the trigger and then cock it again to get the next shot. You get five shots all together."

"That's remarkable," she said, "and very advanced."

Slowly, he released the hammer, clicked it back to the safe position, and laid the Paterson on the table. Into his jacket pockets he plunged his hands as he explained, "I've got spare cylinders here. I'll leave one with you." On the table he set a loaded, five-shot cylinder. "If you had to, do you think you could handle this repeater?"

"It looks easier than a rifle," she admitted. "But, what is the spare cylinder for?"

"That's how you reload it." He popped the locking pin loose with a special tool, pulled the barrel, and slid the repeater's cylinder into his hand. "You drop in a fresh cylinder just like this, put the repeater back together, and then you get five more shots. The cylinder takes some time to reload, so I carry lots of loaded spares." He slid the parts across the table and said, "Now, you try it."

She fumbled the loaded cylinder into the frame. "This is amazing," she said. Into place she pushed the barrel, the opposite from how he had taken it apart. Then she inserted the locking pin. "You know," she observed. "If I had one of these when we were ambushed two days ago, I could have stopped those Comancheros."

Boots lay his hand on hers and she lifted her eyes from the repeater to his eyes as he continued, "You have to set the locking pin, ma'am. If you don't mind, I'll show you." From her hand he took the repeater and rapped the side of it against the table. "Like this," he said. "Otherwise, it'll shake apart while you're shooting it."

"So," she asked, "Do you usually carry two of these, Mister Boots?"

"Yes, ma'am. They give me ten shots before I have to reload and that gives me an edge against the marauders. I can shoot while I'm riding my horse and that's something they can't do. My horse doesn't like the noise much, but he's getting used to it."

"So, this makes your rifle obsolete, doesn't it?" Molly asked.

"Not obsolete. I still use it for long range, but everyone knows y'all can't shoot a rifle while you're riding a horse, and that's where I usually am when I'm in a fight, riding my horse. I used to dismount to shoot my rifle and I only got one shot. It takes too long to reload and a lot of folks have been killed while they were reloading. I'd rather not do that."

Across the cabin she aimed the repeater, holding it up with both hands clasped around the butt. Closing one eye, and looking along the top of the barrel, she observed, "Yes sir, Mister Boots. I wish I would have had this a couple days ago."

He finished grinding the oats, finished a second cup of coffee, and a handful of jerked beef. Standing, he tipped his hat and said, "Been a pleasure, Missis McCracken. You just stay inside and keep that door barred. If anyone comes up that lane while I'm gone, blast them with that repeater, unless it's me when I come back. I'll whistle or something. Three short whistles, how's that? See y'all this afternoon sometime."

"I'll have fresh flatbread waiting for you, Mister Boots."

"Obliged, Missis McCracken, I'll look forward to it."

Through the window Molly watched him saddle his horse and clop away. The morning grew hot and the afternoon was sweltering, but she kept the door barred, even with a fire in the chimney and bread in the pan. The open windows provided a small amount of breeze.

The first cake of flatbread cooled on the table while the second cooked in the chimney. Around her head she tied a strip of bandage cloth and used it as a sweat band, for the heat in the cabin was nearly unbearable.

When the sun began to set that evening, she lit the candle on the table and began to worry. Boots had not returned, as he had promised. She could hardly resist the aroma of the flatbread, wanted to save it for him, but finally seated herself at the table. Breaking off a piece of bread, she enjoyed the aroma and took her time eating it, allowing it to melt in her mouth. The second loaf she saved for Boots, placing it up on the shelf.

Nighttime chased the twilight from the fields and the cabin remained hot inside. She wanted to leave the windows open, but was frightened alone. At the front window she reached out to close and bar the shutter when she heard horses coming up the lane, not just one or two horses, but several of them, thundering toward the cabin.

THE BLACKBERRY PATCH

MOLLY GRABBED THE Paterson repeating pistol from the table, crouched behind the window and laid it over the windowsill. Several riders galloped into view. Comancheros, she thought, and she feared the farm was about to be looted. In her hands the repeater leapt unexpectedly. The flash startled her and the report hurt her ears. Instantly, the horsemen pulled back their reins and dropped from their saddles to the ground, as if they'd all been shot at the same time. They patted their horses away and ran for cover behind trees, a plow, and the shed. She heard them cocking their weapons and she ducked down.

A hushed voice asked, "Is anyone hit?"

Someone replied, "No one's hit. Want for us to rush the cabin?"

"Just hold up," a gruff voice answered. "Let's work our way around back first. Get them surrounded and cut them off, so they can't get away."

"There's smoke coming out that chimney," someone else added.

"We'll burn them out if we have to," the gruff voice continued. "Let's get them out in the open before we go running up there."

Someone kicked the door. Molly scooted her back against the wall, as the hinges creaked and dust puffed out between the door-boards. The bar held and the door did not open. She heard them backing up to take another run at it. Then they rammed it, bending the door in at the corners. Molly screamed, pointed the repeater at the door and cocked it.

"I think I heard a woman scream in there," the man outside the door called out.

"I heard it, too," the gruff voice yelled. "Hey! You in the cabin! Can you hear me?"

"Yes," Molly responded.

"I'm Zacharias Thaxton of the Texas Rangers, San Antonio. We're using this here farm as our station. Why are you shooting at us?"

"It was an accident, sir. I didn't think this thing would go off so easy."

"What's your name, anyways?"

"Molly McCracken."

"Don't do no more shooting or nothing until we talk, okay?"

"Okay."

"I'm coming up there, so don't shoot."

"You're gonna get your head blowed off, Zach." The man outside the door scoffed. "I heard her cocking a gun."

Someone else added, "I think that would make him a lot easier to get along with."

Then they all laughed.

"That's enough out of y'all." Zach walked up, stuck his head in the front window, and gazed down into the muzzle of Molly's shaky repeater. Raising his bushy eyebrows he said, "I only got one head, ma'am, and I'd like to keep it, if y'all don't mind."

She could hear the others laughing yet outside, but cautioned him, "I'd like to see your hands first."

Lifting his hands above his head, he surrendered to her. Politely, he lifted his hat and held it above his head. "Y'all have to excuse us, ma'am. We don't usually come back here and find pretty women-folk like yourself hanging around … Say, do I smell bread cooking in there? How'd you managed to wind up here, anyways?"

Molly lowered the repeater to her lap and briefly explained everything, concluding that Mister Boots had left that morning to look for the Comanchero's camp.

"Mister Boots?" Zach chuckled. "That's a new one on me. Never heard no one call him Mister Boots before." He lowered his hands. "You mind putting that repeater on the table? It's making me nervous. And, could y'all open the door? The boys are hungry, and you got all the jerked beef in there … Don't suppose y'all can spare some of that bread I keep smelling?"

"I promised it to Mister Boots. I mean Captain Williams."

"Rider coming," a voice called from outside.

Molly heard three short whistles, and then Boots Williams galloped up the lane. She heard him pull up at the corral with the other Rangers. Opening the cabin door, she stepped outside, and noticed that the Rangers were starting a fire in front of the shed. Zach let himself into the cabin, and then strolled out with the sack of jerked beef. As they talked, she heard Boots's voice rumbling among them.

Stepping out where they could see her, their chatter fell noticeably silent. Their eyes seemed to catch and hold on her. Checking the buttons on the floppy red shirt she'd found in the clothes pile, she made certain they were all properly fastened.

Zach fanned his hat at the Rangers and scolded them, "Don't you boys know enough to stand up and show this lady some respect?"

Standing, they doffed their hats.

Boots motioned to her and said, "Come on over here and meet the boys."

Taking a few cautious steps, she paused and replied, "First, I'd like to apologize for shooting at you."

"No need," Zach piped. "Boots here says he told y'all to blast anyone who came up the lane. You were just doing what he said. He didn't know we'd be getting back two days early. No one got hurt."

"I'm relieved for that," she said. "But, I didn't intend to shoot at you. The gun just went off."

"Then it's my fault," Boots admitted. "That repeater has a touchy trigger. I should have warned you not to put your finger down on it until you're ready to shoot." He motioned to her again. "So, don't be shy. Come on over here. Seems like you already know Zach. This over here is Doyle, then Noah, and Asa. That young feller over there is Alsey."

Zach made her think of a kindly grizzly bear, someone she could trust. Asa gave her a flashy smile when her eyes met his and immediately she acknowledged that he was unusually attractive. His demeanor suggested that he liked the ladies and was one whom she should keep her distance from. Doyle and Noah had a tough mystique, the kind that comes with hard times. Alsey, however, looked more like a naïve teenager with a fuzzy jaw rather than a Ranger, and she recognized him from when she fled Gonzales.

"I talked with you once, Alsey. Do you remember me? It was the first day after we left Gonzales? I was in the wagon with my sister and brother-in-law, and I asked you to get Captain Williams for me so I could speak with him about my husband, Emmet."

"Oh, yeah." He smiled open-mouthed at her and scratched the scruffy beard under his chin. "That was you? I remember. You were a lot more … A lot more …"

"More lady like?" Molly suggested. She was embarrassed by the men's clothing she had to wear, but thankful to have them, and she knew her hair was a disaster.

"Yeah. You had more …" He bugged his eyes for lack of words and puffed out his cheeks.

Zach laughed at him adding, "She had more common sense, a lot more than you'll ever have."

At this the Rangers hawed at Alsey.

Molly spun around, not sure whether she had been insulted or not and walked off toward the cabin.

"Wait, Missis McCracken," Boots called her back. "You have to excuse Alsey here. He don't know any better. He's just a kid. The only reason we keep him around is for entertainment purposes."

She turned back toward the fire.

Boots flung a pebble at Alsey and grumbled, "Apologize to her!"

Alsey lowered his head and shuffled his feet. "Ma'am, I'm … I'm …"

"It's all right, Mister Alsey."

Boots motioned to her again. "I found your brother-in-law this morning, Missis McCracken. It looked like he put up a good fight, too. I also found two Comancheros he killed. I buried him proper. That's why I'm late getting back."

"Much obliged, Mister Williams. That gives my conscience some considerable ease."

"I noticed that they took your wagon. The tracks look like they took it down to Matagorda. I figure they wanted to load it up with supplies and smuggle them up to General Urrea."

"Do you think they are the same ones that went up Gotier Trace last night?" Molly asked.

"I'm sure of it and I found their camp, too. The one you escaped from. I'd say there's about twenty-five of them. They've got nine or ten horses, and two wagons. They're probably twenty miles or so up Gotier Trace by now."

"Did you see any sign of my niece, Amy?"

"No ma'am. I found lots of tracks, but no sign of the little girl."

"Are you going to look for her?"

"The first thing we have to do is keep the Comancheros from smuggling supplies up to Urrea. You agree with that, don't you? It's our duty."

"I understand." She hung her head.

"I brought something back for you though." He nodded toward the corral.

Behind his saddle she noticed that he had tied a chest and it had a rounded top. "My sea-chest!" she cried out.

"Your things were all over the road. I also found a spinning wheel, loom, and quite a few farm tools. I figured they must be yours. The Comancheros dumped everything in the road and took your wagon. Your trunk was laying there open, and it looked like the wind blew everything into the brush. I picked up as much as I could fit back in the trunk and brought it back with me. I'll put it in the cabin for you."

Knuckling away tears, Molly thanked him saying, "You don't know how much this means to me, Mister Williams. I thought everything was lost. Most of those things belonged to my sister and brother-in-law. That's all I have left from them. Thank you very much for bringing that chest to me."

"Missis McCracken, I also want to explain that if the boys hadn't come back early, we wouldn't have a chance of stopping those Comancheros from smuggling supplies. So, soon as we're done eating, we're going after them. I figure before sun up we can catch them and take them by surprise."

"Then, you want me to stay here?"

"Yes, and I'll be needing that repeater I left with you. Those repeaters give us an edge."

"How will I defend myself if I have to?" Molly asked.

"We know the Comancheros have moved up the road. So, you won't need to defend yourself from anyone before we get back and we should be back tomorrow afternoon."

"Yes, Mister Williams. I understand."

Zach took a half-smoked cigar from his pocket, pulled a twig from the fire, lit up and mumbled, "Might not get another chance like this."

The others agreed.

"Wait here a minute," Boots said, and then dashed into the shed. When he returned, he had in his hands two dueling pistols, which he presented to Molly, butt first. "Take these, Missis McCracken. These are my old pistols. They're good firearms and dependable. I carried these for a long time and they served me well. You shoot them the same way you shoot the repeaters. The only difference is you get one shot apiece instead of five. That might be all you need. Go ahead, take them."

"Obliged, Mister Williams." She lifted the pistols gingerly from his hands.

Untying the sea-chest, he carried it to the cabin, while the Rangers prepared to leave. Once inside, he instructed her further, saying, "Keep those pistols with you even when you're sleeping. It should only take us half-a-day to do what we have to do and get back here. Nothing can happen in half-a-day."

She nodded and tucked the pistols in the waist of her floppy trousers. When he rode out, he paused in front of the cabin and glanced back at her. From the doorway she watched him lift his hat and say, "There's a blackberry patch out behind the pasture if you're interested."

She waved him on.

Leaning forward, he kicked his horse into a gallop, and behind him the other Rangers galloped down the lane to Gotier Trace.

Alone again, she closed and barred the door. At the chimney she stirred the coals and added a small piece of wood to keep the fire alive. Boots hadn't touched his flatbread, and she had a longing for it, but left it for when he returned tomorrow afternoon. The cabin was too warm, but she closed and barred the shutters anyway. It was dark and she was afraid. There wasn't anything else to do but turn in for the night.

Mourning doves cooed a wakeup song outside when the sun came up. The cabin had cooled down, quite comfortable in fact. Sunlight sifted through the spaces between the logs and around the shutters. She wasn't in a hurry to get out of bed and behind her head she laced her fingers, looking up into the rafters, recalling a morning like this when she walked Amy to the pasture back home in Gonzales. Amy loved to look at the spring flowers. Cupping them in her upturned hand with the stems hanging down between her fingers, she'd study every intricate detail of each petal, breathe deep and then say, 'They're booty-full, Aunt Lolly.'

Smiling through watery eyes, Molly noticed for the first time that her muscles didn't ache as much this morning. Lifting her bandages, she blinked until her vision cleared and examined her arms and legs. Her scratches had hardened. In fact, she felt pretty good. Swinging her feet to the floor, she concluded that this farm would be a pretty good place to live under other circumstances. It reminded her of home, but it didn't seem likely that she would ever see Gonzales again.

The other loaf of flatbread tempted her throughout the day, but she didn't touch it. Instead she munched on jerked beef, made coffee and tolerated the gnawing in her stomach, which wouldn't go away.

Her eyes rested on the sea-chest and she decided it was time to see what was inside. Opening the lid, she was surprised to find almost everything there, although in disarray. Under the clothing she found her mirror. Lifting it, her reflection startled her. Her face was gaunt and pale. Her eyes were sunken back and circled puffy red. On her face she recognized that peculiar look, the look that she had seen on so many other faces, anguish, grief, and furrows of agony. Turning the mirror over, she laid it on the table. She had seen enough.

At the bottom of the sea-chest she found her diary and writing kit, so she spent the afternoon updating it. Then she returned the diary and repacked all the personal items and household goods, folded in Emily's clothes and her black dress. The dovetailed shipping box was still there, the one she'd picked up at the Schauble's wagon when Maria Benson gave birth to her baby daughter. In it she placed the porcelain baby from the king cake and the mask Innis had worn for Emily on Fat Tuesday. Then closing the chest, she shoved it under the table, out of the way.

When her stomach growled she took out another strip of jerked beef from the sack. It tasted like the sole of her old, rotten shoes, hadn't been seasoned or salted, only dried, more like tasso than jerky. Up on the shelf she glanced at that loaf of bread, tempting her yet, and she recalled the breads and pies that she and Emily used to make in the spring after they'd been in the thicket collecting berries. She'd give anything for a fresh pie right now, or just one good home cooked meal.

When darkness had overtaken the cabin, a sense of impending danger overtook her. The Rangers had not returned and she feared that something terrible had happened to them. If she stayed in the cabin, she could be the next target of whoever was out there. She had to leave. But, where would she go? Closing up the cabin, she tried to retire for the night but was unable to sleep. With the pistols tucked in her waist, she lay in bed and prickled up at every sound from outdoors.

A sleepless night gave way to a weary morning. The Rangers had not yet arrived. Opening the shutters, she found that daytime wasn't nearly as frightening as nighttime had been. From the clothes pile she dug out her rotten shoes and put them on. The uppers were stiff and barely attached to the soles. When she tightened the laces, they broke. Knotting the laces, she tied her shoes, and then tore fresh strips of cloth to bind her shoes together, double wrapping them. She had to get out of the cabin, and she had to find something else to eat besides jerked beef.

Outside, the yard was blotched with sunlight, which fell peacefully through the trees. She went to the shed and found everything quiet. Inside she found a length of rope, and used it to secure the waist of her trousers and the two pistols Boots had given her. She decided to wait for the Rangers until that afternoon. If they did not return by then, she would have to leave the farm for her own safety. In the meantime, she recalled the blackberry patch that Boots had told her about, and the thought of fresh berries made her mouth water.

In the cabin she fetched the empty grain-sack and took it out to the pasture. From the path she entered the pasture and was stricken by the mephitis of bovine carcasses now caving in with decay. Unable to breathe, she lifted her shirt collar, covered her mouth and nose, and hurried across the pasture.

By the fence she took a deep breath and noticed a path the owners of the farm had cut into the thicket, probably leading to the river. It was partially grown over but appeared passable. Beyond the path and behind the fence along the back of the pasture she could see blackberries.

Climbing the fence, she found an abundant patch of blackberries and pushed her way in until she was about shoulder high among them. Positioning herself where the berries were sweetest, fattest, and most abundant, she ate about as many as she dropped in her sack, all the while considering where next she would go if the Rangers failed to return.

The afternoon passed and she decided to wait one more day for them. That evening she didn't build a fire and didn't light the candle. She didn't want her presence known to anyone. The Rangers had not returned and she feared for her life. Unsure whether to stay or leave, she finally took a seat in the cabin and waited in the dark with her pistols drawn and resting on her lap. Without realizing it, she nodded off.

In the morning she woke with a jolt, knowing that she had to get away from the cabin. Even if the Rangers returned, it would be too dangerous to wait for them there. Feeling vulnerable and unprotected, the blackberry patch seemed like a suitable place to hide, and she probably wouldn't have known that if she hadn't spent a night and a day in the thicket when she escaped from the Comancheros. From there she'd be able to hear what was going on up at the cabin and she'd know if the Rangers returned.

Upon the table she poured out the grain-sack of blackberries, and along with a portion of them she ate Boots's loaf of flatbread from the shelf. Then she rolled up the grain-sack in a blanket, tucked both under her arm and headed for the blackberry patch. Covering her nose and mouth again with her collar, she crossed the pasture and climbed the fence. Glancing over at the path through the thicket, she decided to follow it and have a look. Maybe, it would take her to the river, and maybe she would find wapato. That would certainly be a welcome addition to her meager food supply. She would fill her sack with them.

A thousand or so paces took her to the river, where she found the banks marshy and thick with wapato. Along the edges she waded, checking first for alligators, then eating the tender wapato shoots, and dropping others into her sack. Pulling the shoots, tubers and all, up from the bottom, she broke off and discarded the thread-like roots, rinsed the tubers in the river and dropped them into her sack.

On a stretch of riverbank she sat and lunched on wapato shoots and tubers in the sun. She'd grown fond of the potato-like tubers back home in Gonzales. Even uncooked she liked them. They were fleshier in the fall and winter, but edible all year around and they were waiting to be pulled up and eaten at any time. Then, feeling safe for the first time in two days, she took a much needed nap.

Rising from her nap, she continued to forage until her sack was heavy. Slinging it over her shoulder, she searched for the path back to the farm. Most of the day had been taken with foraging and napping, and the sun was dropping quickly toward the western horizon behind her. The time had come for her to return to the safety of the blackberry patch and wait for the Rangers. She was afraid to return to the cabin.

Locating the path, she walked up toward the farm. When the pasture came into view, she could hear horses clopping around the cabin. The Rangers had finally returned, and she was relieved. Crossing the pasture, she entered the path to the cabin, picked up her pace, and ran to greet them. She could hear them shouting.

"Alguien está aquí! No hay comida en la cabina."

The Rangers didn't speak Spanish. Instinctively, she dove into the bushes at the edge of the path and listened. Were they Comancheros? She could tell by the sound of their voices that they were inside the cabin and talking.

"Busque si hay ganado en el pasto!" someone outside ordered.

Many of them mounted their horses and galloped up the path from the cabin toward the pasture, and toward her. Wiggling further into the brush, she was thankful that it was almost dark. Behind a stand of seed stalks and briars she got a glimpse of them in the gloaming light. Though she could hear their horses galloping, they looked to her as if they were barely moving. Their uniforms were black and fastened together with a double row of brassy buttons. A red stripe lined the sides of their trousers. Their cuffs and collars were also red. On their heads they wore black top hats, which reminded her of the top hats she had seen in New Orleans. Their hats were adorned with ornate brass insignias on the fronts, long black bills that shaded their eyes, and a plume of feathers rising above. Chin straps kept their hats from blowing off, and bushy moustaches and beards flowed over their chin straps. Sashes of white were slung over their shoulders, and at their sides swung scabbards and swords. Muskets were slung over their backs. The sight convinced her that the riders were not Comancheros. They were General Urrea's cavalry.

The cavalrymen rode into the pasture and pulled up. Molly crawled further into the brush, believing that if she couldn't see them, they couldn't see her.

"Todos están muertos!" one of them yelled.

She couldn't understand what was said, but understood that the soldiers were not happy with what they had found in the pasture. Turning their horses, they rode back to the cabin.

She broke away toward the blackberry patch, leaving her wapato and her blanket behind, running as fast as she could. The cloth on her shoes was soggy and stretched. In stride, her shoes flapped open and clapped shut, but she ran fleet of foot and rolled over the fence into the blackberries. There she lay silently, watching and listening. It seemed that no one had noticed her, not yet anyway.

By now, she surmised, the soldiers were enjoying the Ranger's jerked beef and coffee, and they were eating, no doubt, the remainder of her blackberries, which she had left in a pile on the table. They knew that someone had been staying at the cabin and she knew what would happen next. They would be looking for her. Crawling in among the blackberries, she was thankful for the bandages yet on her arms, legs, and knees, and for her trousers and long sleeves, which caught in the thorns, but protected her from them. Standing up where she was hidden from view, she watched as horsemen rode out from the yard. Spreading among the trees, they searched the brush. More of them rode into the pasture and searched behind the carcasses. Three of them dismounted and entered the path to the river. She was far enough from them that their presence did not worry her. To be safe she dropped out of sight onto her knees.

Deeper into the thicket she crawled. Finding a game tunnel, she followed it until she was in a desolate place. Then taking a seat in a soft patch of grass, she pulled the collar of her shirt over her face to keep the mosquitoes away, and prepared to wait out the soldiers. The thicket provided the only real safety she'd known. The soldiers couldn't follow her there and wouldn't find her if they tried. She listened carefully, could hear them shouting at each other, and could hear hooves clopping back and forth in the pasture.

She waited quietly as the thicket darkened, and then she heard a crackling sound, which piqued her curiosity. Cocking her ear she tried to listen.

THE BRAZOS

SMOKE ROLLED OVER the pasture, choking Molly as it engulfed the blackberry patch. Breathing through her shirt collar, she stood and beheld the cabin ablaze behind a stand of trees. Flames roared from the rear window and caught the eaves on fire. Moments later the roof caved in and flames leapt into the air, showering the dark sky with bursts of sparks. Then another flame roared up from the shed.

Suspecting that the soldiers might be trying to lure her out, she decided to spend the night in the thicket. Smoke drifted above her, but at ground level the air was fresh. So, she lay back, interlaced her fingers behind her head, and watched the sparks drift over and burn out in the sky.

In and out of sleep she drifted until a cold north wind stirred her grassy somnolence and morning brought a cold drizzle to the thicket. Standing, she could see a smoldering heap beyond the trees where the cabin had been. Cautiously, she crossed the pasture, pausing to watch and listen. There was no sign of Urrea's cavalry anywhere. They had left the night before. When she reached the yard, she heard the whinny of a horse. Pivoting on the balls of her feet, she ran for the safety of the thicket.

"Don't run!" someone ordered. "Wait right there!"

Molly looked where the shed had been, and among the ashes stood a tall man covered with black soot. Rain dripped from the brim of his hat, and steaming rags hung from his hands.

"Mister Williams?" she whispered under her breath. Little more than a stranger to her, she couldn't be happier to see anyone at this moment.

Running to him, she threw her arms around him and said, "Mister Williams, I was afraid that something terrible happened to you." Realizing that her embrace had been presumptuous, she stepped away from him.

Steaming rags slipped from his hands to the ground, as he replied. "I'm sorry it took so long to get back. You've probably been scared to death."

"Scared? Yes, I was scared, but not scared to death, Mister Williams. Not yet anyway … Did you come alone? Are the other Rangers with you? I hope nothing happened to them."

"They're fine. I sent them up to Harrisburg to rejoin General Houston and his troops. We're withdrawing from this area. There isn't anything more we can do here now that all the folks have left. The boys went on ahead. I told them I'd catch up after I found you."

"I'm glad you came back, Mister Williams. I was going to leave a couple times but I wasn't sure where to go. I knew it wasn't safe to stay here … It's been four long days."

"Again, Missis McCracken, I apologize. What happened is the Comancheros were all the way up to Missis Powell's Tavern with those supply wagons before we caught up with them. By the time we got there, General Urrea and his troops had burned the place to the ground."

Gasping, Molly said, "Oh, no! That means something happened to Missis Powell! What happened to that dear woman?"

"I don't know, Missis McCracken. We broke off our pursuit at that point and retreated."

"What about her boys, Mister Williams. Couldn't you do anything? Couldn't you rescue them and take them with you?"

"It looked to me like there were at least a thousand troops there, Missis McCracken. They had supplies, cannon, and cavalry, and there were only six of us. When Urrea's cavalry spotted us, about a hundred of them gave chase. It took us the best part of three days to shake them off. It's a good thing we know the country better than they do, or they would have had us." Across his perspiring face Boots dragged his sleeve, smearing black soot as he continued, "I've been riding all night. When I made it back here, I found that the cavalry got here before I did and burned the place down. I was afraid they caught you."

"I hid in the thicket until they left," she replied. Glancing behind him at a smoldering heap, where the shed had been, she asked, "Were you looking for me in there?"

"Here in the shed?" he asked in return, looking back. "I had some things in there. I guess they're not important anymore. I checked the cabin first. I sure was hoping I wouldn't find you in there. Then I was afraid they'd taken you with them." Gesturing toward the yard he asked, "Did you see your things over there?"

On its side the sea-chest laid with its contents scattered from the burned out cabin to the edge of the woods. "I saw it burn," she cried. "The cabin burned all night last night. I thought everything was lost." Running to the yard, she began to retrieve her belongings, and stuff them into the sea-chest.

"Let me help you." He gathered everything he could find into the sea-chest, everything except the tableware, which the soldiers had apparently taken. Closing the top he said, "We need to get away from here. Think you can ride?"

"Yes, I can ride."

Behind his saddle Boots lashed the sea-chest, and explained, "We'll have to go cross country. Gotier Trace is too dangerous. Urrea's cavalry could pop up anywhere." Cinching tight the knots around the trunk, he gestured to Molly that she should mount up, and said, "It's going to be a rough ride."

Placing her foot in the stirrup, she swung her leg over, and scooted up on the back ridge of the saddle, and in front of the chest saying, "I'll manage."

Mounting up in front of her, he turned his head and warned her, "I might have to fight with you up here. So, prepare yourself for it." Nudging his horse down the lane toward Gotier Trace, he paused to glance up and down the road. Then he crossed east into a vast, swarded plain dotted with stands of trees and thickets.

"So, where are you taking me?" Molly asked.

"Do you have any kin I can take you to, or friends you can stay with?"

"No kin. Not anymore. I had friends in Gonzales, but I don't know where they are now, or even if they're alive."

"Then I'd like to take you where you'll be safe, over to Liberty."

"Liberty? That's quite a ways, isn't it?"

"It's two-and-a-half days by road, probably four or five days cross-country. I've got kin over there you can stay with, my Aunt Ruthie. She's my ma's sister. Nice old gal. You can't help but like her. She runs a ferry-boat across the Trinidad, calls it Tuck's Landing. I go there whenever I can. She's the only kin I got left."

"You'd do that for me, Mister Williams? I don't understand. You don't even know me."

"I know you need help, Missis McCracken. That's enough."

"How do you know if she will take in a destitute refugee like me? I don't have any money to buy food or pay my keep."

"I can't say that I know that, Missis McCracken."

"Where else can I go?"

"Don't know that either. Let's just take one thing at a time. First, let's take you to Tuck's Landing, okay?"

"Okay."

Riding cross country in cold drizzle, Boots put dozens of stands of trees between them and General Urrea's cavalry. Searching midday for a place to rest and for water for his horse, he entered a thicket, and met a swarm of gnats, which landed and then flew away, taking with them tiny patches of flesh. Molly pulled the collar of her floppy shirt up over her head to protect her face and neck from them.

Riding on through the briars, Boots swatted the pests. When he stopped beside a shallow creek they were swarmed by mosquitoes. He helped her down and she immediately realized how lame she was. Hobbling around stiff-legged and swatting mosquitoes, she kept moving until feeling returned to her legs. The back of his saddle had been like a bumpy ride on the edge of a split-rail fence and she'd gone numb from the hips down.

"Sorry," he apologized. "I knew the back of my saddle would be a rough place to ride."

"I'm fine," she assured him. Her hips felt out of joint. Leaning against the nearest tree, she tried to rub the tingle out of them.

"You're shivering. Are you cold?" he asked.

"I am now," she replied. Wedged between him and the sea-chest, she had kept warm. Now the drizzle was taking away her warmth, leaving her chilled.

Glancing upward, he observed, "Looks like the sky's breaking up. The sun will be out soon and warm things up."

She almost laughed at him, saying, "You should see your face. It's all black with soot."

"Maybe that will keep the mosquitoes off me," he speculated. "The important thing is to keep moving until we're safe, whenever you're ready that is."

"I'm ready."

Stopping occasionally to rest, graze, and water the horse, they rode until the sun dropped behind her. Ahead she noticed a strip of green on the horizon. When they reached it, twilight had surrounded them, and they crossed a road.

"You're not taking the road?" she asked.

"I'm not taking any chances," Boots replied. Winding into a forest of Pecan trees and swatting mosquitoes, he took them to the steep banks of the Brazos River and pulled up.

Several stone throws wide, the river appeared deep enough for a sternwheeler, like those Molly had seen in New Orleans. Rain had brought debris down the surging middle, piling them into massive jams. Limbs and tree trunks caught where the water was shallow and caused her to wonder how they would ever get across. She didn't ask. "It's getting dark," she observed.

Boots dismounted, helped her down and helped her hobble around until feeling returned again to her legs. "I see plenty of wood lying around," he noted. "Do you feel up to making a fire? I'll go out yonder and see what I can get us for supper. Are you hungry for supper?"

"Yes, very hungry."

Under the pecan trees she gathered deadwood, as Boots sauntered out of sight. The fire was blazing when she heard a shot in the distance, maybe a mile or more away. She was certain it was Boots, but she wasn't taking any chances. Drawing her pistols, she withdrew into the brush and waited where she felt safe.

Darkness settled around her and the fire dwindled into a bed of coals. It seemed like hours had passed before footsteps crunched in the brush close by. Into the dim glow of the coals he stepped, holding a turkey by its feet, its wings spread out and dragging on the ground.

"Saw this one roosting," he explained. "It was an easy shot." Looking around, he asked, "Molly? Are you here?"

"I'm here," she answered from her hiding place. Crawling out with cocked pistols in her hands she said, "I'm not taking any chances either."

His smile faded quickly and he said, "You're taking a bigger chance than you think, crawling around with those pistols cocked."

Standing, she used the muzzle of one to push a tendril of auburn hair from her forehead. His eyes opened wide and he dropped the Turkey. Reaching with both hands, he clasped them over the pistol and said, "Let me help you with that." Jamming his thumb in front of the hammer, he released the trigger and reset the hammer to the safe position. "The other one too," he said.

Lifting the other pistol to him, she inadvertently pointed it directly at his midsection. Ever so gently, he pushed the muzzle aside with his forefinger so that it pointed away from him, and then relieved her of it, saying, "You have to be careful where these are pointing. They can blow the top of your head off, or blow out my spine. I'd stand funny if my spine gets blown out."

"Sorry, Mister Williams."

"We'll work on that later … I have to admit. It sure is different having a woman along." Raising one of the pistols, he aimed at the nearest pecan tree, and said, "I'll bet this one won't even fire," He pulled the trigger. The pistol clicked, and nothing happened. To his side he lowered it. Raising the other one with his other hand, it fired, throwing a flame that lit up the pecan tree, and smacked a chunk of bark off the trunk about the size of his hand. At that same moment the pistol hanging at his side also discharged on its own, spewing fire into the ground and splattering both of them with dirt.

Molly jumped away screaming, "What happened?"

"These old single-shooters don't like the rain," he explained. "They tend to hang fire and sometimes they won't fire at all."

She'd fixed her gaze on the spent pistols in his hands and asked, "And, you want me to defend myself with those?"

"It depends on how wet they are. You were out in the rain last night and all morning. You can't depend on any firearm that's been out in the rain that long. The only way to keep them dependable is to clean them, dry them and reload them. We can do that tomorrow. Right now let's make a spit and get this Turkey roasting."

Molly built the fire up again as he skinned the bird, removing feathers and all. Stripping the bark from saplings, they threaded the bird onto one of them, bent other saplings over it, and bound everything together with reeds. Then across a set of forked, upright sticks he set the bird over the fire. Seating himself, he added to the fire a handful of green twigs and leaves. Steamy, white smoke filled the campsite and he said, "That should keep the mosquitoes away for awhile."

Molly seated herself across from him and asked, "Do you like to roast a Turkey when you and the other Rangers are out on campaign?"

"I'm doing this for you, Missis McCracken. Usually, we don't eat until we get back to the station. A fire like this can give away our position."

"And you're not worried about this fire?"

"Well yes, I'm concerned about it, but there aren't any unfriendlies in this area, none that I know of. You can't be too careful though. We won't sleep in the same place where we cook and eat our supper."

"What if you're on campaign for two or three days? Will you go hungry for that long?"

"We usually carry jerked beef to take the edge off. Mostly we have to keep our guard up, have to keep ourselves ready to fight at all times. That's what we're here for. That's what folks depend on us for. But, folks have been known to invite us in for supper from time to time, too."

"That doesn't sound like much of a life, Mister Williams. I can't imagine why you would want to live like that."

"Well," he said, "It was like this. I only had enough money for a horse and a gun, and I didn't want to be a bandit."

Molly smiled but wasn't sure whether she should believe him or not.

He smiled and then he laughed. "That's what I like to tell folks when they ask. Actually, I came fresh out of surveying school in Nashville. I went to work in San Antonio. Problem is, when they sent me out on assignment, I was always getting shot at by folks who didn't want us around. The Mexican government had withdrawn their troops from the frontier and folks had to organize their own defense or get driven out by the Comanches. It wasn't just the Comanches either, there were lots of tribes coming out of the States and laying claim to land the Mexican government had sold fair and square to the settlers. There's lots of folks that don't want us to be here in Texas, Missis McCracken, not just Santa Anna and the Mexican government. I got tired of being shot at, and I got tired of seeing innocent folks get pushed around and murdered. So I decided to do something about it and that's how I got where I am. I became a Ranger."

"Will you be a surveyor again, when the war is over?"

His mouth straightened and his gaze fell into the fire.

She didn't understand how her question could have offended him, but apparently it did. "Don't you want to have your own land and your own home?" she asked. "That's everyone's dream, isn't it? That's why folks come here, to buy land. Don't you want to have a family to go home to? Don't you want to have someone to grow old with?"

"I had that once," he mumbled.

She could barely hear him and wondered what sort of dark secret he was hiding behind those ghost-blue eyes.

Again he mumbled, "I'll be dead anyway."

Molly held her breath. What he said didn't make sense and she pleaded, "You have an education and a career to look forward to."

"That part of my life is over."

Raising her knees, she wrapped her arms around them and continued, "I can tell that something hurt you deeply, Mister Williams. You don't have to tell me … I don't want you to tell me. But I can see it's wounded you in ways that haven't healed. You're carrying it around inside you, aren't you? Just like I carry the loss of my sister, my brother-in-law and my niece. There isn't a day that goes by that I don't suffer for them. But dying won't heal the pain. It would just make me unable to feel it anymore."

He didn't answer.

Fearing that she'd offended him again, she looked away. Dropping her forehead onto her knees, she wished that she hadn't said anything at all. Then her stomach growled.

He laughed, apparently hearing her stomach and asked, "The smell of this bird is killing you, isn't it? I know it's killing me. About another half-hour and it's going to heal both our pains." Again he laughed.

To her knees she spoke, "Mister Williams, what I said, I shouldn't have said that. I'm sorry."

"You don't have to be sorry. It's something I decided quite some time ago. I'll keep doing what I'm doing until the end comes. There's no going back for me. It's the way I chose. It's the way of the Rangers, the way of Texas, and now it's my way."

From her knees she lifted her eyes to him and commented, "Then that makes you a very dangerous man, Mister Williams."

At this he turned his eyes from the fire to her and half smiled. She understood him, and he knew it. The look on his face conveyed his satisfaction with her assessment of him. That he was, indeed, a dangerous man.

Then he said, "You remind me of my Aunt Ruthie, the way you escaped from the Comancheros. Aunt Ruthie would've done that, crawling off into the thicket to get away from them. Then you took a shot at the boys, but she wouldn't have missed. And, the way you gave General Urrea's cavalry the slip." He shook his head and laughed. "What made you think of going off to hide in the blackberries anyway? Anyone else would've done something stupid, like hide in the shed, or crawl under the bed."

"I was afraid to stay in the cabin. That's the first place anyone would look."

"You say you were afraid. Then you went outside, so nobody could get the drop on you. That takes gumption. You were listening to what your fear was telling you and you had the gumption to act on it."

"I'm not like that at all, Mister Williams. I was afraid. That's the only thing. I was afraid when I escaped from the Comancheros, and I was afraid when I hid in the blackberries."

"Everyone is afraid, Missis McCracken. The difference is what folks do about it. What you did took courage. Someone else would have done something stupid, and got themselves killed. You've got courage. It's in your blood, same as me. I can see it in you."

No one had ever seen anything good in her before, except Emily, and she'd never thought of herself as courageous. A tingle went up her spine as she thought about what he'd said.

Watching her intensely, he smiled and added, "What I said, I shouldn't have said that. I'm sorry."

Was he mocking her? Molly covered her face and laughed, for she understood his humor. Regaining her composure, she looked again at him and asked, "Does Aunt Ruthie know how you feel about the Rangers?"

"We've talked about it. She asked the same questions you did and I gave her the same answers I gave you."

"She knows you plan to die this way?"

"There's more to it than that …" His smile became reflective and softer as he continued, "Remember when you saw General Urrea's cavalry, when they came to the farm? Do you remember what they were doing?"

"They were in the cabin, talking. Then some of them rode up the path where I was hiding and rode into the pasture."

"How long were they in the pasture?" he asked.

"I don't know, an hour maybe."

"They were only there for a minute. I'm sure of it. Did you feel quickened?"

"That's a silly question. I was afraid. I couldn't feel anything when that happened." She recalled how slow they seemed to move.

"Yes you could. It just never happened to you before. You said you ran across the pasture with the soles of your shoes flapping. Could you do that now?"

"I … I don't know. You should try running sometime when your shoes are coming apart."

"I don't have to. I know what happened. You were quickened. That's what I call it. Something clicked inside you. Maybe, fear set it off. Call it what you want, but things that only take a couple minutes, seem like they take hours. Things that take a couple seconds seem like minutes, and things that seem impossible become easy. I've experienced more in two minutes when I was quickened than most people experience in a lifetime, and it's happened to me hundreds of times."

"That's a strange thing you've just told me, Mister Williams, a frightening thing."

Into the turkey he jabbed his Bowie, twisting, and he exclaimed, "It's done. You still hungry?"

In silence they ate their supper. Then they crushed out their fire, and moved their camp. When the sun came up, they ate what was left of the Turkey. Boots had hung the carcass in a tree to keep scavengers away. Molly had never felt so utterly exhausted, or so utterly satisfied in her life. After breakfast, she wanted to lie down and cover up with his blanket for a nap, but he wanted to cross the river.

"How are we going to do that," she asked.

"We'll have to swim."

"It's too far across. I can't swim that far."

"We'll make a raft to keep our things dry. I'll tow it across. You can lash yourself to the raft. It will be a lot easier for you that way. I'll swim with my horse, done it lots of times. First thing though, we need to take those pistols of yours down to the river and wash them out before the powder corrodes them."

Down the steep bank to the water's edge she followed him. He removed the barrel from one pistol and she removed the other. On his knees he lowered the breach of his barrel into the water. Using the ramrod and a scrap of cloth like a plunger, he was able to pull water into the barrel through the primer nipple and then expel it out again.

Scrubbing her barrel, she plunged it clean, dried it, reattached it to the pistol stock and reloaded it, copying everything that Boots did.

"All right," he said. "Let's get busy and build a raft with that driftwood over there. We'll have to lash it together with reeds. I don't have enough rope to both tie a raft together and tow it across the river."

She gathered reeds while he stacked drift wood in crisscrossing layers, hacking them to length with his Bowie and tying them. When the raft was finished, he placed their weapons and supplies in her sea-chest with her belongings and tied it atop the raft. Then into the water he led his horse, about knee deep, attaching his rope to the pommel and to the raft. Leaving a tail rope dangling behind the raft he explained, "Tie this around your waist in case you have trouble hanging on. When I pull you out into the river, kick your feet to help push the raft along. That will take the strain off the horse. Okay?"

"Okay, Mister Williams."

Wading into deeper water, he led his horse by its bridal. When he reached swimming water, he took hold of the saddle's pommel and kicked his feet. The rope tightened and pulled the raft away from the bank. Molly was underway, tied to the end of the rope, holding on to the raft and kicking as hard and fast as she could.

Farther out, she could see the current bulging up and rippling down the center of the Brazos. Boots was almost into it, and when he reached the current, it swept him and his horse downstream. Toward the opposite shore he angled his direction and used the current to help propel him across.

Upstream, she could see something drifting around the bend toward them. It looked like a floating brush pile, but she wasn't sure. He was about a third of the way across and had plenty of time to avoid the debris. Ahead, he seemed to have taken a more leisurely pace, and she had to admit, it was almost an enjoyable swim.

Glancing upstream, she realized that what she'd thought was a brush pile was actually a whole tree. Caught in the middle current, it was sluicing down the river much faster than she'd guessed. Judging by its speed, she determined that it would collide with Boots about the time he reached half way across. "Mister Williams!" she screamed. "Mister Williams!"

He could not hear her.

She screamed and thrashed her feet harder, but all she could do was watch, as the tree caught up with Boots and rolled him and his horse under water.

EPILOGUE: TOO MUCH EXCITEMENT

THE ATTIC WAS dimming with sunset and it had become very warm. Mom handed the diary to me. Then lifting the back of her hand to her forehead, she told me that she'd had too much excitement for one day, it had given her a headache, and she was hungry. I glanced over at my wife, and she nodded her agreement. Watching Mom, I thought I was beginning to see Molly's mannerisms in her actions, and it made me smile.

I suggested that we should go over to the Rusty Rooster restaurant in Gonzales and have supper. Both of them liked the idea, so we put everything back in the trunk, closed it, and climbed down the narrow stairway from the attic to the kitchen. After locking up Grandma's bungalow, we piled into the moving van. It was getting dark and I had to admit that I was weary and hungry too, mostly from packing and toting boxes all day. But I could have sat and listened to Mom read that diary all night.

The meal was great and Mom wanted to go home when we were finished. She's in her seventies and I couldn't blame her for wanting to go home. I suggested we could come back and finish packing tomorrow, but she insisted we should not work on Sunday. That was her tradition. She had felt that way about working on Sunday for as long as I could remember. I reminded her that the moving van was due back tomorrow, on Sunday. Then she gave in, and agreed to come back to Grandma's bungalow tomorrow afternoon after church. That sounded pretty good to me and to my wife. So, I handed the diary back to Mom and drove her home to San Antonio.

After we unloaded the moving van, my wife and I called it a day. When we were in our home I asked her what she thought of Molly's diary. She said she thought it was very well written and couldn't wait to hear the rest of it, and she was watching me in an odd way as she answered my question. So I asked her if anything was wrong. Studying every intricate detail of my face, she was looking for Molly in me.

"Thanks a lot," I said. "Molly would be almost two hundred years old. Are you telling me I look like a two-hundred-year-old woman? How do you know I don't look like Boots?"

"No way!" she replied.

~~~~

Here ends Runaway Fever, Volume 1 of the Black Dress Trilogy. I hope you enjoyed it. If so, please visit the retailer where you purchased it and kindly leave a review. Thank you. KT.
~~~~

SELECTIONS FROM *Tuck's Landing* BLACK DRESS TRILOGY VOLUME 2

THE NEXT MORNING began with a tap on the door. Molly's eyes refused to open, but a persistent tap forced them open. "Yes," she said sleepily.

"I've got breakfast ready downstairs." The door had muffled the older woman's voice.

"I'll be down in a moment, Aunt … Aunt."

"Aunt Ruthie. It's all right, darlin', y'all can call me that."

"Obliged, Aunt Ruthie, I'll be right down," Molly climbed off the first feather mattress she'd ever slept on and found the yellow dress Aunt Ruthie had left on the vanity for her. Pulling it on she noticed that it was a little tight in the bodice and it hung below her ankles, pretty nice otherwise. Aunt Ruthie might let her hem it up. Her shoes lay in the corner, cracked, rotten, and separated from their soles. Glancing from them to the vanity, she decided to give her hair a quick brushing and go downstairs barefoot. When she stepped from her room into the upstairs hallway she could smell freshly baked bread.

Down the stairs and across the living room, she entered the kitchen. In back she could see a sunroom full of windows overlooking the Trinidad River and Aunt Ruthie standing by one of them sipping a cup of coffee.

The older woman was taller than her, rangy and long of arm and leg. Taking a seat at a long table she smiled at Molly and said, "Coffee's on the stove, darlin', and there's bread on the counter. Help yourself."

In the morning light Molly had a better look at Aunt Ruthie, her face gaunt and angular. Very old, she looked to be probably in her mid-forties. Her hair was gray, sprinkled with white, and tied into a bun on top of her head. Pieces of hair had fallen astray, floated around her head and jiggled when she talked. The folds under her chin smiled as she smiled at Molly, and her eyes had squinted into happy arches.

Filling a cup with coffee, Molly sliced off a thick piece of bread, slathered it with butter from a wooden dish and took a bite. As she enjoyed the fresh bread, she looked around the kitchen and considered Aunt Ruthie fortunate to have a stove to cook on. She didn't have to crane pots in and out of a chimney. At the end of the counter Molly noticed a pitcher-pump and basin and smiled at such a modern convenience. She'd never seen such a thing inside a house. Aunt Ruthie could pump water in her kitchen and didn't have to carry it from outside.

"I can see that this place has been good for you already," Aunt Ruthie added. "That yellow dress is pretty on you. It don't look that good on me anymore, not since my hair went gray." Glancing down at Molly's feet she asked, "Y'all need shoes, too, don't you?"

"My shoes fell apart," Molly explained.

"I've got extra shoes," Aunt Ruthie informed her. "We'll fix y'all up with something."

Pulling out one of a dozen chairs surrounding a long, polished oak table, Molly seated herself. Glancing out the windows, she could see across a covered back porch to the river crossing and ferryboat below. A wagon, horses, and passengers were aboard, and Klaus was pulling them across as Molly remarked, "The view from here is spectacular."

"Klaus can pull folks across in about ten minutes," Aunt Ruthie explained. "The other hands take twenty minutes or more."

"You have others working here?" Molly asked.

"Justin and Manuel," Aunt Ruthie replied. "They live in the bunkhouse out by the barn. There's more work here than Klaus can keep up with by himself, and they're both good hands."

"I wasn't expecting anything like this." Molly turned her eyes from the window to Aunt Ruthie. "I haven't seen glass windows since I was in New Orleans. And look at this door." Standing, she swept her hand over the door leading out onto the back porch. "I've seen panel doors like this in New Orleans, but only in mansions, when me and my sister were working as seamstresses. This is a mansion, isn't it?"

Aunt Ruthie sipped her coffee and replied, "This house was part of a plantation before Foster got himself killed."

"Your husband?"

"My dear husband cleared the fields and built this place. If you want more bread, just help yourself, darlin'. Make yourself at home. You belong here now."

"I love your bread," Molly complimented her.

Her smile never left her face, as Aunt Ruthie continued, "I bake it fresh every morning so the smell will get the men hungry, and get them out of bed early so they can be on their way. The sooner they're out the better I like it. They should be coming down any moment."

"What men?" Molly asked.

"They're overnight boarders," Aunt Ruthie explained. "I rent rooms mostly to teamster drivers when they're passing through. Fits in good with my ferryboat business, don't you think? Most are on their way from New Orleans to the lower settlements and back. Right now freight hauling has all but stopped because of the war. Lately, I've been getting a lot of settlers passing through. They don't usually stay long and don't usually have no money. If they need to spend the night, I let them camp for free in the marshalling area up on top of the hill. Once in a while I get some government dignitaries, they seem to like it here, but I haven't had any lately. I got the only place in a hundred miles with a hot bath, a feather mattress, and a home cooked meal."

Molly nodded, and when Aunt Ruthie raised her cup, she noticed her forearms, strong for such a frail looking woman. Sinews and veins stood out on them. Her fingers had a certain grace to them though, long, but callused. This woman is no stranger to hard work, she thought, but neither was Molly. "What can I do to help around here?" she asked.

"I've got plenty of help with chores. Klaus and the farm hands do the heavy work, running the ferryboat, and working the fields. I tend the cattle and do the cooking, housekeeping, and gardening." Aunt Ruthie took a deep breath and sighed.

Molly determined then that she should find ways to help while she was here. Then she asked, "So, what happened, Aunt Ruthie? What happened to Foster?"

"Foster Tuck," Aunt Ruthie began, "was a good man. They don't come no better than him. It's a shame what happened. We built cabins and put up a barn. Then we cleared as much land as we could that first year, put in a garden, too. The second year Foster had about five-hundred acres put into cotton and it was a barn buster. He had lumber shipped down to build this house. Things were going along just fine after that. We put another two-hundred acres under the plow, and Foster wanted to get all the rest into cotton. It would have made us rich."

"Sounds to me like you were already rich, Aunt Ruthie."

"Well, let me tell you about rich, darlin'. It ain't the land, or what we put into it, or what we take out from it that makes us rich, it's the folks that does the puttin' and the takin'. They're the ones that make us rich. I'd give everything I have right now to get my Foster back. He got took away from me, and my heart is still aching for him. When I lost him, I lost everything. You may as well have cut my heart out. Y'all might look at me, and think I'm rich, but inside I'm a pauper, poor as dirt."

"So, what happened?"

"Well, he wanted to put all that land under the plow. He bought more horses and more equipment for clearing, plowing and planting. Problem was there weren't enough hands to do everything he wanted to do. He decided that he had to buy slaves. He didn't want to, but all the other plantations had slaves, and they were expanding faster than him. So, one winter him and some of his friends went off to New Orleans on a buying tour. A couple weeks later they came back and said they had been ambushed and robbed by John A. Murrell himself and his gang of freebooters, and that Foster had been killed.

"Boots was thirteen when that happened, and by the time he was fifteen he didn't want to farm, didn't want anything to do with cotton. I sure felt sorry for the dear youngin', tried to get him to accept things the way they were and move on with his life. Finally, he decided he wanted to become a surveyor. He sold his pa's land and used the money to go off to the Davidson Academy in Nashville. I sold my land, too, except for the house and a couple hundred acres. Bootsie sold me the landing and ferryboat. Things worked out pretty well after that."

"When did Boots get married, Aunt Ruthie?"

"What made you think he got married?"

"He said he had a home and a family once. He said everything was gone."

"I think he was talking about his ma and pa and his little sister. He's holding a lot of feelings deep inside about what happened. He might have let you get a glimpse of it, but usually he don't let folks see what's inside of him."

"Am I asking too many questions, Aunt Ruthie?"

"Of course not, darlin'. Would y'all like me to take you for a look around? We can talk some more while you get to know the place."

Pulling on and tying a pair of shoes, Molly toured the outbuildings and the cabin where Klaus and the farmhands lived, and then Aunt Ruthie took her across a mowed lawn overhung with shadow-laden pecan trees. Behind her Molly glanced at Aunt Ruthie's whitewashed, two story house with rows of double hung glass windows, a broad and deep front porch, and the bench-like swing that hung from the ceiling, where she'd sat the night before. From there they walked up the lane and across the Atascosito into a rutted marshalling area where wagons had lined up, and where folks waited for their turn on the ferryboat. Alongside the road a bell hung from a post and crossbeam so that folks could call the ferryboat.

Pointing down to the river, Aunt Ruthie said, "Looks like Klaus is bringing folks across with a wagon right now. Looks like a freight hauler. Folks ring the bell when they want to get on the ferryboat, and Klaus has one on board to ring back at them, telling them to come on down and get aboard. We can't have folks going both ways up and down that hill at the same time. Would y'all like to ride the ferryboat?"

Aunt Ruthie took Molly down the steep grade to the dock and on board with Klaus, the ferryboat operator. Molly noticed that the boat was fitted with a plank deck of oak and side rails, and it was about a third the length of the sternwheelers she had seen in New Orleans. Fore and aft gates were latched while away from the docks. Klaus opened one or the other, allowing passengers to embark and disembark when the boat was secure.

Above the docks on opposite sides of the Trinidad stood oaken beam structures that held large wooden pulleys bigger than wagon wheels and axles. Around the pulleys a hemp rope fed out to the ferryboat. The rope was thick enough to secure a ship, and from the bottoms of the pulleys it attached fore and aft to the ferryboat. From the tops of the pulleys it spanned the river, and threaded through a smaller set of pulleys on the ferryboat railings, allowing the rope to slide across a deck span of about twenty paces, where Klaus could pull or walk with it.

Wanting to give the rope a try, Molly discovered that her hands were too small to close all the way around, but she was able to tow the ferryboat about a quarter-way across before her muscles gave out. The teamster driver aboard was patient with her slow progress, but seemed to be taken up the whole time with gawking at her yellow dress. He offered to help tow the line, but Klaus stepped up and took over.

After the teamster disembarked, a family drove their wagon and a team of horses on board. Klaus closed the gate, and once again Molly attempted to tow the line as the ferryboat drifted away from the dock. Slowing with each tug, she then tried folding her arms over the rope for a better grip and walking with the rope rather than pulling it, but her legs soon gave out as well.

Stepping down from his wagon, a man complained, "I ain't got all day to get across this here river. Let me pull that rope for y'all."

Molly gave him a sideways glance and let loose of the rope. Opening her hands, she looked at the blisters that were forming on the pads of her fingers and palms. "You're right," she admitted. With the tow rope no longer in her hands, her wrists, shoulders and back began to throb.

Klaus stepped in front of him, and said, "Let mm … me do that."

The man looked at Klaus in an odd way, then he mocked him by asking, "You sure y'all know which way to pull on that there rope?"

Heartily, the man's youngsters laughed at Klaus.

Then Molly spoke up in his behalf saying, "Why don't y'all get back in your wagon and mind your own business."

"Until my rig rolls off the other side," the man insisted, "this here ferryboat is my business."

Klaus jerked the rope so hard that the man staggered backwards, fell to a sitting position on the deck planks, and went speechless. His youngsters and his wife held their peace as he jumped to his feet, and scrambled up onto his wagon.

Beneath his beard Klaus smiled. When he saw Molly watching him he bobbed his head, and continued bobbing it until the ferryboat bumped into the dock on the other side. He opened the gate, and the man cracked his whip, driving his family up the hill.

"You handled that very well," Molly commended Klaus.

"Sometimes the things a man duh … does says more than the th … things he says."

"That's very wise of you, Klaus. Anything else you might have said out there would have just made him get madder."

His cheeks brightened, and his head continued to bob.

Across the river the bell rang. On top of the hill Molly saw a teamster waving at them, and he seemed anxious to board. Changing direction, Klaus prepared to pull the ferryboat over to pick him up, but Aunt Ruthie took Molly back to the house.

The next morning Molly put on her floppy shirt and trousers and helped Aunt Ruthie with morning chores. During the afternoons she worked on the ferryboat with Klaus. In the evenings she changed into the yellow dress Aunt Ruthie had given her, brushed her hair into a fountain of auburn curls, and socialized on the front porch with the houseguests.

Three months on the ferryboat gave Molly a remarkable hardness she'd never known. Her wrists and arms grew strong. Her back and shoulders felt like they were knitted together with strands of steel. Veins and muscles stood out on her wrists and the backs of her hands. They began to look to her like Aunt Ruthie's wrists and hands. Turning them over, opening and closing her hands, she admired the progress she was making.

After supper she went out to the barn for her evening chores and heard the bell ring for a tow, but didn't give it another thought. She was off for the evening. Then she heard a popping sound on the river.

Realizing that what she had heard was the pop of a pistol, she became concerned and ran out for a closer listen. Rifles crackled, six or seven of them. Dashing toward the house, she met Aunt Ruthie.

Bounding down the front porch steps, Aunt Ruthie said, "Sounds like someone's getting impatient. Guess I better go down there and see what's going on."

"I'll go, too," Molly offered.

Across the yard Molly dashed with Aunt Ruthie, until Manuel emerged from the lane and met them. He gasped, "Men ring bell to cross river. I am towing ferryboat to get them, and I see man. I know this man. He is Comanchero in alley behind mercantile. With him there are many more men. So, I think it is not good for me to take ferryboat to get him and bring more men over here. I take ferryboat back to Klaus. Then one of the men, he climbs on rope and crosses river to take ferryboat away from us, so Klaus he shot him."

Rifles crackled from the river again as Justin ran in from the fields, raising a cloud of dust as he skidded to a stop. Down the lane Aunt Ruthie dashed toward the road and extended her arm so that Justin, Manuel and Molly would not run ahead of her.

Down the riverbank at the dock Molly could see Klaus hunched behind a piling, and in each of his hands he wielded a dueling pistol. Across the river the Comanchero's rifles crackled. Their rifle balls splashed into the water next to him, and one splintered the piling he hunched behind. Aunt Ruthie whistled to get his attention and when he turned, she motioned him away from the dock.

When the shooting stopped, he stepped away from the piling, glanced up at Aunt Ruthie and then turned to watch the Comancheros reload their rifles. Aunt Ruthie whistled again, bared her teeth at him and motioned forcefully for him to get away from the dock. Up the hill he bounded, surprisingly agile for such a large man. Molly noticed that another Comanchero had climbed out on the rope, and he was pulling himself, hand over hand, toward Tuck's Landing.

Aunt Ruthie yanked Klaus out of the road when he reached her. Motioning everyone together she said, "I'm going to stay right here and keep an eye on them. Looks like they're fixing to commandeer my ferryboat. We have plenty of time before that man gets across the river and takes the ferryboat back to get the rest of them. So, I want y'all to go up to the house and get all the rifles you can find. Bring them here. Hurry, but don't let them see you. I don't want them to get any ideas about what we're up to, okay?"

Searching frantically in every closet and corner when they reached the house, Molly and the others also went out to the barn and gathered up all the rifles they could find. Some of the houseguests loaned their rifles, and two of them wanted to join the fight. One was a chunky man with chubby cheeks and a trim, black beard, who Molly had seen before. Wielding a rifle, she returned with the others to Aunt Ruthie.

The ferryboat was now across the river at the opposite dock, and it was a considerable distance from where Molly stood at the top of the hill. She guessed four or five hundred paces, too far to shoot a rifle, but the distance didn't prevent her from recognizing the first Comanchero on board. A bead of perspiration trickled down her cheek as she watched him. That face, she thought, she would never forget that face.

CPSIA information can be obtained at www.ICGtesting.com
Printed in the USA
BVOW03s1104240713

326734BV00002B/4/P